NO
PLACE
TO
BURY
THE DEAD

NO PLACE TO BURY THE DEAD

A NOVEL

KARINA SAINZ BORGO

Translated from the Spanish by Elizabeth Bryer

An Imprint of HarperCollins*Publishers*

Excerpt on page vii from *Pedro Páramo* © 1955 by Juan Rulfo and Heirs of Juan Rulfo. English translation © 2023 by Douglas J. Weatherford. Reprinted with the permission of the publisher, Grove Press, an imprint of Grove Atlantic, Inc. All rights reserved.

Excerpt on page vii from *Antigone* in *Three Theban Plays* by Sophocles, translated by Robert Fagles. Translation copyright © 1982, 1984 by Robert Fagles. Used by permission of Viking Books, an imprint of Penguin Publishing Group, a division of Penguin Random House LLC. All rights reserved.

Excerpt on page vii from *The Odyssey* by Homer, translated by Emily Wilson. Copyright © 2018 by Emily Wilson. Used by permission of W. W. Norton & Company, Inc.

NO PLACE TO BURY THE DEAD. Copyright © 2021 by Karina Sainz Borgo. English translation © 2024 by Elizabeth Bryer. All rights reserved. Printed in the United States of America. No part of this book may be used or reproduced in any manner whatsoever without written permission except in the case of brief quotations embodied in critical articles and reviews. For information, address HarperCollins Publishers, 195 Broadway, New York, NY 10007.

HarperCollins books may be purchased for educational, business, or sales promotional use. For information, please email the Special Markets Department at SPsales@harpercollins.com.

Originally published as *El tercer país* in Spain in 2021 by Lumen.

FIRST HARPERVIA EDITION PUBLISHED IN 2024

Designed by Janet Evans-Scanlon

Illustration: Texture on page iii © Nadejda / stock.adobe.com

Library of Congress Cataloging-in-Publication Data has been applied for.

ISBN 978-0-06-321387-6

24 25 26 27 28 LBC 5 4 3 2 1

To my people, always.

"You ever hear a dead man moaning?"
  she asked me.
"No, Doña Eduviges."
 "All the better."

> —Juan Rulfo, *Pedro Páramo*,
> translated by Douglas J.
> Weatherford

When you died I washed you with my hands,
I dressed you all.

> —Sophocles, *Antigone*,
> translated by Robert Fagles

They wanted only to stay there,
Feeding on lotus with the Lotus-Eaters.
They had forgotten home.

> —Homer, *The Odyssey*,
> translated by Emily Wilson

NO
PLACE
TO
BURY
THE DEAD

I came to Mezquite searching for Visitación Salazar, the woman who would bury my children and teach me to bury those of others. I walked to the ends of the earth, or where I believed my own world had come to its end. I found her one May morning beside a stack of burial chambers. She wore red leggings and work boots, and a colorful scarf was tied around her head. A halo of wasps wheeled about her. She resembled a dark-skinned Madonna astray in a dump.

On that arid parcel of land, Visitación Salazar was the only living soul. Her dark lips framed white, square teeth. She was a beautiful Black woman, shapely and willful. Her arms, strong from cleaning the graves, gleamed in the sun. It was as though she were made of oil and jet instead of flesh and blood.

Sand had muted the light, and wind needled in our ears, a moan that seemed to rise through fissures in the ground. That breeze was a warning, a dense, strange dust storm, like madness or pain. The end of the world was a mountain of dust, formed from the bones we had left behind on our journey here.

At the entrance was a sign daubed with thick brushstrokes: THE THIRD COUNTRY. It was an unofficial cemetery, home to the dead that Visitación Salazar buried in exchange for goodwill alone, sometimes not even that. Almost all who had been laid to rest had only the date of their burial on the slab. Their meager tombstones were engraved with scribbles made in fresh concrete: the rough scrawl of those who would never rest in peace.

Visitación didn't even turn to look at us. She was on the phone. The device was in her left hand; in her other were plastic flowers, which she planted into the recently churned mortar.

"Yes, honey, I can hear you!"

"Are you sure she's going to talk to us?" Salveiro murmured. I nodded.

"I can hear you, mamita!" she continued, "I was saying there are no more vaults. Ayyyyy! You're breaking uuuuup!" she cried, tragicomic.

"Will she ever get off the phone . . . ?"

"Hush, Salveiro."

"Tell the man to wait!" she cried, finally addressing us. "The dead are patient! The dead are in no hurry whatsoever!"

Another gust of wind seared our skin. The land surrounding Mezquite was a skillet piled high in thistles and laments. It was a place where there was no need to drop to one's knees to do penance. The penance that had brought us here was enough.

That was how it was in The Third Country, a border within another border, where the eastern and western mountain ranges met, as did the living and the dead, good and evil, reality and myth.

The plague and the rains arrived together, as bad omens do. The cicadas fell quiet, and a tumor of dust materialized in the sky until it started leaking drops of brown water. In contrast to the calamities we had suffered before, this one shattered our memories and desires.

The plague attacked memory, disorienting it first, then eroding it. It spread quickly, and the older the person, the worse they were afflicted. The elderly fell like flies, their bodies unable to withstand the assaults of the first fever. In the beginning, it was said to be contracted from water, then there was talk of birds, but nobody could explain the amnesia epidemic that transformed us all into specters and filled the sky with vultures. It made us inept, swaddled us in fear and oblivion. We wandered aimlessly, lost in a world of ice and fever.

Men went out into the street to wait. For what? I never found out.

We women did whatever we could to keep despair at bay: We gathered food, opened and closed windows, climbed up to the rooftops, swept the patios. We gave birth heaving and shouting like those madwomen whom no one offers even a sip of water. Life concentrated in us, in what we, until then, had been capable of holding on to, or pushing out.

My husband got infected too, but it took me some time to realize. I misattributed the first symptoms to his temperament. Salveiro was a man of few words. He was reserved and felt little curiosity beyond his own affairs. When I met him, he worked at his family's garage, loosening nuts with a lug wrench, or lying alongside a hydraulic jack to fix some malfunction in the innards of a run-down truck. I often passed by the dark premises but never paid too much attention to what happened inside. One day I went in because I needed engine grease for the locks at home: a pot of 3-in-One, something to lubricate the latches, but Salveiro offered to come take a look.

"It's not the latches. It's the timber. It's being eaten away by termites, that's why the doors won't close, see?" He showed me a small mound of fine wood particles.

He came back the same week to inspect the roof and the rest of the house. He surveyed the house in its entirety. Checking whether a beam was a breeding ground for gnats, whether the table legs hadn't been finished properly or the table itself had been ineptly sawn. He went from one end to the other, a tool in hand. He sanded this and hammered that. Everything he set his eyes on stopped creaking or rasping, as if he could repair things by sight alone.

"And who is this, Angustias?"

"The tire fitter's son, Papá. He offered to fix the window sashes and frames."

After each visit, we offered him a beer to thank him for his trouble. He took a seat beneath the tamarind tree and didn't mind being quizzed.

"Why don't you leave the garage and do this instead? You have a knack for it," said my father, but Salveiro took a swig without answering. "Angustias has a hairdressing license. You could try taking a course. If you had a certificate in carpentry, you could run your own workshop."

"I just opened a beauty salon," I said, drawing attention to myself. "It's two blocks from here. Come for a haircut, and I'll tell you about course prerequisites?"

He showed up the next day. He was wearing clean trousers and a freshly ironed shirt. The sleek skin of his face, smelling of aftershave, contrasted with his grease- and oil-smeared arms. After massaging shampoo and lotion into his scalp, I steered him toward a chair, settled a cape over him, and used my best scissors to trim his locks. The damp tufts collected on his shoulders.

In the end, Salveiro didn't take the course, but he kept showing up three times a week to deliver one thing or repair another.

"Angustias, he looks like a tree trunk, but if you like him . . . ," my father murmured in my ear before smiling for the only photo we took of ourselves in the doorway of the courthouse where Salveiro and I were married.

My husband was a good man. He was gifted in bed. He knew how to touch me with the same patience he showed whenever he manipulated wood. He said little, but I didn't mind. And that was the problem: I never imagined that his silence had something to do with the lethargy already sweeping the streets, with the cloud of weariness that was burying the city alive.

My mother baptized me Angustias. Instead of a name, she chose a blow. Anguish. For her, the world had always been silent. For that reason, whenever someone calls out "Angustias!" I think of her resignation as a voiceless woman. In some respects, I resemble her. I know how to withstand my fair share. I am always braced for misfortune. I speak her language.

Until Higinio and Salustio were born, I hadn't considered leaving the city, but then things took a turn for the worse. Our boys had come into the world prematurely, and they had a heart defect. Together, they didn't even clear four and a half pounds on the hospital scales. Their small, wrinkled hands barely stirred. Their fingernails were purple, their eyes squeezed shut. Life had decided to loan them for a while.

For three months I sat beside an incubator, fearing the worst. Though no one could guarantee that their hearts would hold out, the doctors decided to operate. They survived, while the city crumbled beneath the filthy rain that washed the pavement. I didn't want my sons growing up in a ghost valley that everyone else was abandoning.

"We're leaving."

Salveiro glanced at me, stung by the snake of despondency, then returned to tinkering with bits of a broken blender.

"I want to leave," I repeated.

"You think it's that easy?" He set the screwdriver down. "The preparations take time."

"You can stay if you like. I'm leaving."

We sold our furniture, bedding, and tools, as well as the mirrors, chairs, and hair dryers from the hair salon. I only kept a small pair of hairdressing scissors, which I slipped into my pocket and still carry with me to this day. The money we raised was enough to cover part of our fare.

We left the capital with our sons tied to our backs. We embarked on a journey of more than five hundred miles, half by bus and the other half on foot. We would reach our destination after crossing eight states in the eastern mountain range, as well as the three that still lay between us and Mezquite, a town on the border named after a bush that makes good firewood.

We had only a few coins, three mandarins, and a backpack containing a change of clothes, two baby bottles, and packets of powdered milk that we made in whatever stream we came across. Along the interstate, a road that crossed the central range, we kept on, forming a parade of "walkers," which was what people called us refugees of the plague.

We adapted as best we could. Any gully was fit for washing and cooking. Before resuming our trek, I tied my hair into a topknot, so the boys wouldn't be bothered by loose strands brushing against their faces. I made a promise to myself not to cut it until we arrived at our destination, wherever that might be. Salveiro trailed me, shooing the mosquitoes with broad swats of his hands, and collecting bits of wood that he slipped into his pockets. With each day that passed, I felt I was leaving him a little farther behind. I grew convinced that if I turned around, I would find him collapsed on the path like a tree devastated by termites. Many nights I imagined waking alone, in the middle of nowhere, with two boys to carry around. I dreamed I was walking on all fours, transformed into a lioness capable of knowing where the gazelles were fleeing simply by lifting its nose to the wind.

From a distance, we could make out the tents that the sol-
diers had pitched along the border. The mass of people in search
of food and medicine could be seen from half a mile away. Anyone who had money left by bus, the rest did so on foot, carrying
what little they could. Abandoned along the wayside were refrig-
erators, lamps, and saucepans, which someone else would steal
as exchange for food.

When we reached the first checkpoint before the bridge, a
soldier detained us to inspect our papers. He was young and slen-
der. His hair was poorly shaven, marked with the telltale nicks
always left by those who don't know how to use a razor.

"Where are you headed?" he addressed Salveiro first.

"The eastern mountains . . ." My husband seemed more absent
than usual.

"We're in the eastern mountains, citizen."

"He meant western," I interrupted. "We have family there. We
want them to meet our sons."

The sergeant looked at me skeptically. I handed him my ID
and Salveiro gave him his. I presented our birth certificates too,
but he only glanced at those. All his attention was focused on the
twins. He eyed them with curiosity. First Salustio, cradled in my
husband's arms, and then Higinio, who slept with his head resting
on my shoulder.

He wanted to know their ages. I explained they were born
prematurely, that this was the reason they looked small. He nodded and vetted our papers a final time. His wife had just given
birth to a girl, premature too, he explained as he noted our names
in a pad.

"What's her name?" I asked.

"Whose?"

"Your daughter's . . ."

"She doesn't have one yet."

He went inside the control booth and returned with a safe conduct pass for crossing the border. "Vaya con dios," he uttered, and handed us the scrap of paper.

That was how we got away, Salveiro, the boys, and I. God never did choose to accompany us.

My boys died in Sangre de Cristo, the first hamlet across the eastern mountains. They left this world much the same way they entered it. Higinio first, then Salustio. I took them to three hospitals in search of a miracle, but nobody was able to revive them.

We wrapped them in towels and carried them like so until we found two boxes. My babies were so small that together they would have fit into just one, but that didn't give us the right to cram them in like shoes. Salveiro wanted to leave them in the morgue until we raised enough money to bury them. I refused. They were dead, but they were my children, and I wasn't about to leave them piled in a fridge full of nameless corpses. At the morgue, taped to the door of a rusty cooling chamber, I found a sheet of paper: "Twenty-five fetuses, seven to inter per bag." The note was written in black marker.

I brought my sons here for the same reason I had left home with them tied to my back. I believed I could save them from the sickness, and from oblivion. But instead of outrunning death, I only ushered them to its door. At night, when the roads were overrun with thieves and opportunists, we searched for a bed at one of the shelters that were popping up everywhere. They were not safe, but they were good for resting weary heads.

In those hovels made of concrete blocks and tin roofs, women and babies were lumped together, all of them feverish with hunger. Disoriented elderly, abandoned by their families before they made the crossing, were there too, as were children whose parents had disappeared along the road. The orphans who didn't die became delinquents or did other families' bidding in exchange for a tip. They were lost souls, transients caught between one world and the next.

Very few of those setting out on the journey had any idea of what they would face. They walked for hours, thick blankets wrapped around them. At nightfall, if they were lucky enough to find a spot, they collapsed on makeshift beds and mats, hungry and shivering in the cold of the páramo, which at that time of year was punishing in the border region.

In the first hamlet across the eastern mountains, a woman my age was in the street, singing to an eight- or nine-month-old little girl in her arms. Occasionally a passerby threw a few coins into the wicker basket at her feet. The little one stirred, about to cry. The woman paused her singing to nibble the little one's fingers and soothed her to sleep. I had no coins to give, nor children to protect. Mine were in a deep slumber from which they would never awaken, lying in a pair of shoeboxes.

In the shelter, I hid them beneath my blanket. One awful woman tried to take them away from me. I pounced on her and yanked her hair, the only thing I could grab hold of in the dark. She whirled around until she managed to free herself, along with one of the boxes. When the cardboard lid toppled to the floor, she cried out in fright. Her eyes, sunken into their violet sockets, shone in desperation. She had been searching for something to peddle—a pair of shoes, perhaps—but had found a dead child instead.

When I recovered the box, I saw she had stolen all the money we had left, as well as the pass we had been given to cross the bridge. Standing before the open door, I watched her flee down the street. I still had a fistful of her hair in my hand.

Twenty miles from Sangre de Cristo was the largest black market on the border: Cucaña, a place where mothers, grandmothers, and daughters went to sell their hair. They entered, their long tresses pulled into buns, and came out with heads shorn and a few bills in hand, though the sum amounted to barely enough to cover three packets of rice.

The most crowded hair salon was Guerreros, a grimy, dingy locale attended by scores of hairdressers with the look of shearers. Outside, fifty or sixty people awaited their turn as if they were about to enter a slaughterhouse. Guerreros resembled a barracks: there were no shampoo stations, just a single row of plastic chairs.

"We'll pay sixty for yours, less for your mother's."

"How much less?"

"Twenty. It's old hair—dull, worthless fuzz."

"Only sixty? But my hair is so long," she complained.

"It's the going rate today. If you don't like it, step aside. *Next!*"

I peeked inside to better hear. Everyone turned to look at my hair, which at the time reached my waist.

"For hair like hers," she indicated me with her scissors, "we pay a premium."

"How much?" I asked.

"Eighty."

I joined the line amid rumblings. Others stared at me as if I wore a gold tiara. I was terrified they might wrench my hair out by the roots, but stayed put. I needed the money. The theft meant we couldn't even afford crackers or water. Two hours later, I stepped inside.

The hairdressers cut the women's hair like horse manes. They held it taut with a comb and brought the scissors as close to the scalp as possible, so as not to waste a single inch.

"Not like that," I stopped her, "you need to start at the back and then cut around the sides."

"What, you're going to show me how? This is no beauty salon!"

"Let me do it."

I removed my scissors from my pocket. I slipped my thumb and fingers into the handles and cut. Locks of hair fell like vines onto the newspaper spread across my lap. When I had finished, I rose without a glance into the mirror, headed for the register, where a woman was removing bills from a steel cashbox.

They paid me seventy, ten less than promised. I took the money and went out into the street.

All the women in Cucaña had the same terrible haircuts. They roamed the place like packs of shorn creatures. I still had two inches of hair at least. The others had not even that.

When there was nothing left to cut or sell, they offered themselves to the truckers. They waited for them in the early hours next to the stands where foreigners and haulers, men who haggled down the rate in the back of their trailers, ate breakfast. Not all women found clients. Those who did got it over and done with as quickly as possible. Then, they went to the restroom to wash up and drink the muddy water pouring out the faucets, and to dole out the money. They peered over their shoulders and spoke in hushed voices, as if words could be stolen too.

Out in the street, young girls and adolescents waited for them, all of them too young to do what the women did. Instead, they spent their time caring for the youngest children. It was hard to tell if they were family, though poverty brought resemblance enough. These small caregivers begged, trying to secure a few coins in exchange for the spoiled fruits they had scavenged from the trash the night before.

All the young ones spent their days in a market where vendors sold products they could not afford. They witnessed quarrels among stallholders, robberies, and altercations. They barely had enough to eat and resorted to cunning to earn what little money they could. In time they learned to thrive too. They couldn't read fluently, they had trouble writing, but they knew everything there was to know about life.

Cucaña was full of people primed to buy and sell. Everything had its price: medicine, saucepans, secondhand clothing, contraband cigarettes, hair, false teeth, gold teeth, furniture, household appliances. . . . Whole lives could be made over by the market's cut-price sales and discards.

I asked Salveiro to hold the boxes containing our boys and went into the restroom, looking for somewhere to change and freshen up. There were no stalls, only three dirty toilet bowls for relieving oneself, partitioned from the washbasins by plastic tarpaulins. There were no rolls of toilet paper or wastebaskets either. I hid behind the plastic curtain and used my second-to-last sanitary napkin.

When I reemerged, two women were talking in front of a broken mirror as they scrubbed their armpits with damp cloths. They stank of sweat and vinegar. I recognized them instantly. Those of us from the eastern mountains didn't need to say a word to one another to know where we came from. To hide, I washed my face with the brown water that trickled out of the rusty tap.

The speakers were young, yet their skin was tanned leather, wrung out by hunger and fatigue. They were whispering something about a dead cousin. This was the first time I heard anyone mention Visitación Salazar. They referred to her as the Tolvaneras woman.

"She arranged a burial chamber for my mother. She even helped us transport her."

"Is it far away, the cemetery?"

"About forty miles, next to the Mezquite dump."

"What did she charge you?"

"She doesn't care about money. She says she's a soldier of God," she lowered her voice even further. "She gets around in a gray pickup. Go find her, and say I sent you."

"And who will cover my shift?"

"We'll work it out. Go on, get going! You can't leave Herminia in the morgue, they do away with the bodies before too long."

They fell silent and warily looked my way, so I left in a hurry. In the middle of a ditch full of puddles and mud, I regretted having bolted. I wanted to know more about this Visitación: her phone number, or at least an address where I could locate her. Annoyed with myself, I returned to the restroom, but the women were gone.

On my way back to the market, I bumped into a girl who looked to be younger than thirteen. She came up to me, decisive. Her slim child's physique hid a body on the cusp of adolescence. Her arms were puny, and her breasts small, stunted by involuntary fasting and exposure to the elements.

"I'm selling tomatoes, want some?"

In one hand she held a wooden stick, in the other, a bag of spoiled fruit and vegetables.

"They're rotten."

"Oh, okay," she said. "So, I'll lower the price for you. You just have to rinse them."

"I don't want them, and I don't have any money anyway." I watched her scratch her head. "Do you know who the Tolvaneras woman is?"

"The one who buries the dead?" The girl's hair was so grimy it hung stiff. "Her name is Visitación Salazar. Everybody knows her."

"Where can I get ahold of her?"

"Right here! She comes every day, early."

She sized me up with suspicion.

"And why do you want to talk to her?"

"I need help."

She sank the stick into the dirt and placed her hands on her hips.

"Around here, all of us need help. So do you want my tomatoes or not?"

"Some other day."

I turned and started toward the market stalls. I found Salveiro in the same place I had left him. He had a lost look on his face, his arms limp at his sides.

"We're going to Mezquite." I snatched the boxes from his hands.

"What for?"

"To find somebody to help bury our sons."

t was before eight a.m. when the phone rang. The mayor of Mezquite was gazing into the mirror, a razor blade in hand. His mustache still sponged with foam, he took the call from Alcides Abundio, owner of Tolvaneras and the richest and most powerful man on the entire border.

"What can I do for you, Abundio?"

"You stupid asshole."

Aurelio cleaned his cheek and adjusted the towel at his waist.

"At city hall there's no end to the people showing up and begging for money. That, or they've come to ask about the madwoman."

"Which one?"

"Who else? Visitación Salazar! The lady who humiliated you with a shotgun intended for small game. Or have you forgotten?"

As if he could.

"My contributions are over!" cried Abundio hysterically.

"Before the plague, things were different, but now . . . well, you can see for yourself. The mountains are crawling with those people."

"The plague my ass! They can all drop dead, but they had better do it far from my land!"

"Don't get upset. . . ." Aurelio Ortiz set the razor blade by the faucet and switched the phone to his other ear, "Did you come by my office?"

"Of course not! Gladys told me."

He wiped the steamy mirror. He was convinced somebody was watching him in the gloom.

"I told her I didn't want any more bullshit at Tolvaneras, but since you're on the campaign trail you don't give a fuck."

Ortiz turned around, searching for whomever or whatever spied on him.

"Aurelio, answer me! I'm talking to you! Governing is easy when you've got my support, yet you can't even do it then!"

"Don't be like that. . . ."

"I'll be however the hell I want to be! Visitación is defying us. The insolent bitch spends all day every day with her dead. She'll soon join them if she doesn't get off my land!"

"Wait and see what the lawyers say."

"Lawyers my ass! I made you mayor of Mezquite so you would look after my interests!"

"Abundio . . ."

"Shut up, Aurelio! And listen carefully: I promised the priest a parcel of land. There are others wanting their cut of the pie, you know who. So long as those graves are there, I can't keep my word."

"Listen."

"Go take care of Visitación Salazar, or I'll skin you alive!" And he hung up.

The mayor mopped his forehead. He was nervous. He didn't want any more trouble with Visitación Salazar, but since the fight for Tolvaneras began, she had encroached a further two and a half acres beyond what she had already stolen. She had appropriated it from old Abundio, from the irregulars' armed command, and from the traffickers, who made a living moving drugs, people, and merchandise. She was screwing them all, and, of course, none of them were amused.

Each had Visitación Salazar in their sights, for different reasons. The most vicious was the priest. Overnight he had been fleeced of the land Abundio had promised him for the construction of a parish house. Furious, he sent for the police first, and then wrote the diocese. He didn't rest until he'd had Visitación excommunicated. He accused her of profaning and usurping the sacrament of the anointing of the sick, then of being a thief, even of witchery. "This shameless woman is stripping the Holy Church of its assets, and the poor of the western mountains of theirs!" he cried, arms outraised, palms to the sky.

But the priest was livid about something else. Tucked into the parochial housing project were plans to set up a bingo hall where he could install the town drunks and swindle them with the aid of coca paste, aguardiente, and bachata. All so they would then kill one another with their machetes. If he induced them to sin, his feat would be eternal.

Aurelio was still troubled.

"Keep your mouth shut, or you'll wake up tomorrow with your mouth stuffed full of dirt!" Aurelio's wife berated him the night he told her what had happened.

"Salvación, don't be like that, I just . . ."

"You work for the old man. And you and your children depend on Abundio."

"Our children, you mean."

She looked him in the eye.

"For once, just this once, be a man. I already do my share, raising two boys while you spend the day traipsing from one town to the next."

Salvación, like Abundio and the rest of Mezquite, ignored the true injustice of those lands. That, or they feigned ignorance, which is the safest way to live in a border town surrounded by mercenaries and traffickers.

"Worry about your own affairs, and don't stick your nose where it's not wanted. Vacate that piece of land without a fight," Aurelio had warned Visitación Salazar on more than one occasion. The last time he tried to talk sense into her, she responded with a few shots into the air.

Nobody at Mezquite's city hall or the police station could tell us what we should do. They had us fill out a form and promised that, if possible, our case would be reviewed the next day. Exhausted, I collapsed onto a metal bench, the boxes still in my hands. How long would this drag on? We would get nowhere without money and a safe conduct pass.

Hundreds of people just like us were walking, lost, lugging flimsy baggage and plastic bags full of worthless belongings. Some camped outside city hall, saving their spot in the long line of hopefuls. The rest had taken to the hills, trying to get by.

We hitchhiked back to Cucaña, where at least people didn't look at us askance, since everybody there looked a little worse for wear. We returned to the shelter and divvied up all we had left to eat: a mandarin and a few crackers. Salveiro stretched out on one of the rickety beds and pulled apart the fruit, eyes on the ceiling. I wasn't hungry. As a comfort, I removed the lids from the boxes and gazed at the twins' sleeping faces.

We couldn't go home, but we couldn't stay there with our dead babies either. I sang, very softly, stroking their heads.

White dove
with the little blue crest
take me on your wings
to see Jesus.

"Quit it, Angustias, they're dead. They're not coming back," Salveiro cut me off.

"What would you know. You're not the one who gave birth to them."

I left the bunkhouse still clutching the boxes and plopped down to watch the sunset next to the generator.

"Did you find Visitación?" I turned around, startled. It was the tomatoes girl. "I just saw her at the market, in the bar. Run, before she leaves!"

"Wait here for me!" I asked the girl.

I darted into the shelter, hid the boxes beneath Salveiro's bed, and ran back, but the girl was no longer there. When I reached the bar, Visitación had left already. I scoured the market until I found the gray pickup everybody talked about. I waited, but nobody appeared. I passed by every market stall asking after her. The stallholders, who at that hour were packing away their goods, barely acknowledged me.

"Have you seen Visitación Salazar? She was here not long ago."

A woman shook her head.

"I'm looking for Visitación Salazar, do you know her? Has she come by?"

No response.

The butcher had seen no sign of her. The woman at his side hadn't either. Nor had the next stallholder, or the one opposite. I circled back to the area used as a parking lot, but the pickup had disappeared.

The hubbub of the market was dying down, and the sellers' hawking was soon substituted by the murmur of dive bars and the crickets, which started their chirping as night fell. Back at the shelter, the skinny tomatoes girl waited for me, seated on the steps.

"Did you get ahold of her?"

I shook my head. I sat down beside her, devastated.

"Who died on you?" She kept pushing her bangs out of her face.

I took my scissors out of my pocket.

"Don't move."

I combed her hair with my fingers, then parted it in two. I gripped the first part between my index and middle fingers and snipped away. Small tufts of fuzz fell to the ground. I did the same with the other section, until it was even.

"That's better, isn't it?"

She nodded.

"I asked who died. Are you going to tell me?"

"My sons."

"All of them?"

"Yes, all of them."

She got up, brushing the clumps of hair from her skirt, and handed me a scrap of paper with a number jotted down. Then she ran off without saying goodbye. I unfolded the note. Written in a clumsy, slanted hand—the nine resembling a vowel, the three an eight—673-842-921.

I spent the last of my coins. The call went through. On the fifth ring, a woman answered.

"Visitación Salazar?"

"The very same."

"My name is Angustias Romero, and I want to bury my sons."

Don Abundio is busy."

"I've brought a few documents," replied Aurelio Ortiz. "Let me through."

The security guard placed a hand on his holster.

"He's attending to several matters." A glib smile spread across his face. "He's with Perpetua. Go back to city hall. He'll be a while."

Aurelio turned on his heel and clambered into the pickup.

"Head into town, Reyes."

Ever since the plague broke out across the border, hundreds of people had arrived in Mezquite, and it made him nervous. They had forgotten their way home, wandering the back roads, starving after traversing the páramo that separated the mountains from the border. Many had lost their minds, and the bodies of those who didn't die hanging from a tree disappeared downstream.

The town could no longer accommodate mass graves where they could be buried. Everybody sought a place where they could lay their loved ones to rest, and the name Visitación Salazar was making the rounds. They flocked to her with the desperation of people who have nothing, not even a place to bury their dead. Her name became legend. Those who venerated her called her a saint; those who loathed her accused her of shady dealings.

Visitación wasn't one way or the other. She didn't perform miracles, nor did she traffic organs like everybody started to say. She was a talkative Black woman who danced, smoked, and drank, like everybody else in Mezquite. She spouted the sorts of things evangelicals do, and she recited her own version of the Old Testament, but she didn't sell people to smugglers, and she wasn't in the business of turning the refugees into slaves, unlike Abundio.

The mayor knew why the old man was in such a hurry to drive Visitación out of Tolvaneras. He wanted the priest to bless his union with an Indian for whom he intended to abandon his wife Mercedes. His wife was an educated woman, slim as a steeple. She no longer lived with him, only visiting town every now and then to play the part of his wife, although even that was something she hadn't done for a while.

After wringing all he could out of Mercedes and her kin, Abundio now intended to reestablish his bloodline with the young woman he christened Perpetua. She had come to Mezquite after the irregulars set fire to the hamlet where she lived. Abundio taught her how to use shoes and forced her to stop eating soil—which was what she had been doing when they found her near Cocito, a small town where horses and drunks sometimes got spooked. People said it was because they could hear the lament of restless souls wandering about.

Aurelio Ortiz didn't believe in such things. It wasn't the spirits. What had truly exhumed these demons was the coke, coca paste, and caña blanca consumed.

etween Cocito and Villalpando cleaved a gorge known as Perla. It lay to the north of the Cumboto River. As the drought persisted, the current dwindled, until scarcely a silver thread linked the estuaries. At the edge of those quagmires, small pools of water formed. Sparrow hawks splashed in them, then rose into the air, fish skewered on their beaks, while scarlet ibises of brilliant plumage foraged along the sandbanks.

Only those who braved the journey to The Third Country on foot happened upon Perla, a torrent enfolded in a landscape that devoured the things it touched even as it made them beautiful. Much was said about that river: that it concealed treasure chests and gold coins; that as its water level dropped, burial sites guarded by tormented souls were revealed; that its currents hid snakes of gold; that in its sands grew seed pearls and mother-of-pearl. A galleon had even come to rest there, claimed the adventurers who navigated its waters in search of relics to make them rich.

Along both banks, miners from the south advanced, ragtag crews that had supplanted the local fishermen. Nobody wanted to fish those waters now that they were teeming with criminals. Equipped with ropes, pickaxes, and wire mesh, the gold prospectors pressed on toward the Cumboto headwaters, where the tributaries that watered the mountains began. They paid no heed to the law because time had inscribed a law of its own on their mercury-swollen gums. When they spat phlegm, they let out crude, bitter words.

They were drawn here by the precious metal nuggets and diamond chips of the Gato Negro caves. For them, a speck of something was enough to justify their pilgrimage. These were people with nothing to lose and everything to gain in that lawless, arid land.

Perla spanned a part of the border that dealt in stolen goods. The treasures people spoke of didn't surface by magic; they had been buried by somebody making a quick getaway, hoping to come back for the treasures later. The gorge's otherworldliness didn't come from its waters' properties but from the way the current could veil things, distort them. And so, ghosts and legends were imagined, to dissuade the treasure hunters.

Exhausted, my feet red raw with blisters, I came to Perla's water to wash my feet, scrub the dirt from my face, and relieve the pain in my ankles, already battered by so many rocks.

"Angustias, the fish are flying . . ."

When I heard that, I shivered. I presumed Salveiro had now entered the worst phase of the plague: a loop of hallucinations caused by the fever. I felt afraid, for him and for me. I could carry two dead bodies, but not three. I stayed silent, my feet submerged.

"I'm telling you, the fish are flying!" he repeated.

An iridescent shoal seethed across the river's surface, making it resemble a saucepan boiling beneath the sun. I rubbed my eyes, trying to make out the details. The fish were a blue hue with capelike fins, which they used to propel themselves across the surface of the water, like a flock of egrets crossing the sky.

The white river sand, shining in the midday sun, created a mirror effect that made it seem as if they were flying. I sank into the water and asked God for a miracle. Beneath the surface, the world sounded soft and distant. For as long as I remained, nothing would happen. Everything would be in its place, and I wouldn't have to keep on. The only reason I resurfaced was for my boys. Someone had to bury them.

I walked back to the river edge and sat down beside my husband.

"Yes, Salveiro, the fish are flying."

We were silent as we gazed around us, in that place where all the ugliness and beauty of the world had come to rest.

Do as instructed, Gladys!"

"There's a line of easterners outside, Mayor. They've been here since five this morning."

"Tell them I'm out!"

"Don Abundio left a message, he said he doesn't like seeing those people out front."

"He told me the same in person."

"Mayor . . . *wait!*"

Aurelio Ortiz slammed the door, attempting to assert an authority he did not possess. He detested Gladys. He put up with her because he had no choice. The woman was more telegraph operator than receptionist: she typed with her index fingers, pressing firmly, as if writing Morse code. She never responded to anyone's greetings, and she pretended she was deaf whenever he relayed instructions.

Gladys's relationship with the Abundios went way back. First, she worked for Reinaldo Abundio, the father, then for Alcides, his son. She was appointed Aurelio's assistant at city hall for one reason: to keep an eye on him. It was how she supported her ten children, snooping for two generations of the same family, washing their dirty laundry.

Alcides, the present Don Abundio, continued his father's patronage of Gladys's brood. They all ended up with good jobs in customs, looking after goods or carrying out simple tasks at his behest. They all showed deference. If he asked them to kill themselves, they would, not out of loyalty, but out of fear that Abundio would do it first.

Taita, as Alcide's father had been widely known, encountered

Gladys on the old sugarcane plantations. Her husband had died at one of the cockfights he often attended. Taita was the main promoter. He was there the day Gladys's husband took a bullet to the chest.

It was an act of revenge, or so said everyone present. The Malay rooster the man presented in the fight skewered the eye of the American rooster Taita had bet everything on. *Bad news*, thought the bookmakers. Rightly so.

Neither survived. Besides the two pecked-to-death fighting cocks, the owners were laid out too. The winner, from a bullet wound, the loser, bled out after somebody stuck him with a knife in the ensuing confusion.

Some swear the old man ordered the killing and, once the commotion died down, bought the widow's silence by seeing to it that her children wouldn't go hungry. But it was simpler than that. Gladys proved loyal because of the power play that turns murderers into patriarchs.

It happened in the golden years, when Abundio Sr. made his fortune paying his farmhands with scrip and trafficking animals in Cucaña. Back then the irregulars, armed troops that controlled those lands, completely dominated the area: They kidnapped and killed at whim, levied taxes on all landholders and factory owners, and started recruiting farmhands among their ranks. The farmhands started to earn more from their guns and the kidnapping ransoms. Once initiated, they underwent military training, which turned them into mercenaries. The irregulars didn't pervert them with cruelty; instead, they simply mobilized the cruelty they had carried inside all along.

Uniformed in olive-green jackets and army boots, the irregulars appeared out of nowhere brandishing their machetes and submachine guns that had originated with the national army. Equipped with the guns of men they had put to death, they patrolled with swagger, tucking their thumbs into their belts. They regarded their neighbors with contempt. Having grown up with these people, now they slew them with relish, spurred by old resentments. They lay waste to hamlets, stole animals, raped at whim, and, dissatisfied with simply killing them, butchered young men. They abandoned the mutilated arms and legs on the road into town, making it exceedingly clear who ruled the area. The irregulars were a ripe opportunity for anybody who knew how to manipulate, and for that reason Taita waited for the right moment to get them eating out of his hand.

A terrible drought, the first of several, brought numerous men and women from the eastern mountains to Mezquite. Abundio senior took in anyone who wandered onto his land, teaching them to use a mattock and draw water from the wells in exchange for food and shelter. If they arrived in good condition, he deceived them by promising to help secure the papers they needed, only to pawn them off to the irregulars as an olive branch. That was how he struck up a long, solid relationship with the guerrillas, one Abundio Jr. still benefited from. He continued to recruit men. No longer to employ them or subcontract them to the area's feed mills as cheap labor, but to offer them to the highest bidder. Selling people was more lucrative. He built his empire on the bones of these people, supplying them to the irregulars at a price, or in exchange for arms.

That was how, thanks to Abundio, new recruits swelled the ranks of the bloodiest patrols in the region. The guerrilla commanders thanked him for his efforts by eliminating his enemies and granting him safe passage to their poppy plantations, where they produced heroin to finance their war against the state. They were killers, but they knew how to concede certain liberties, so long as it remained in their best interest to do so.

We buried our marriage along with our children. I didn't know who was more dead, the twins or us. Even our clothes weighed heavily. The whole journey, I didn't let go of the boxes containing my boys, and rarely did Salveiro threaten to take them. Time and dust fused my babies to my hands, just as once they had been cradled within my womb.

Even though she had seen us arrive, Visitación Salazar didn't stir. She stayed as she was, shovel in hand before the open grave where the dead twins who Salveiro and I begot out of love, boredom, or desperation would soon be laid to rest.

"Visitación Salazar?" I asked.

"Yes?"

"My name is Angustias Romero."

There was a stony silence, barely disturbed by the roar of the wind.

"Is that your husband?"

"Salveiro, yes."

"Is he the little ones' father?"

I nodded.

"And why aren't you saying anything now? A second ago, you wouldn't stop making a fuss; your wife was mortified. Did the cat get your tongue? Or did you bite it off in shame?"

I interrupted.

"In Cucaña I was told you could help us bury our sons."

"That's correct, my dear. Your boys will find eternal peace here."

"But you just said there are no graves available," said Salveiro.

"In The Third Country, no child is ever denied a burial." Visitación paused dramatically before proceeding. "How many are there?"

"Two. They're twin boys," I answered.

"Are they inside those boxes?"

I looked at the ground, burning with embarrassment.

"Let me see them," she ordered.

She approached a shed made of concrete blocks and sheet metal, the only shade available in that hot, dusty hell. Grabbing some keys hanging from a nail, she opened the door of the gray pickup.

"Angustias, you ride shotgun. Talkalot can get in the bed, with the twins."

"You're not going to take a look at them?" Salveiro stayed where he was, in the middle of the shed.

"Let's see, Talkalot, you want me to look at your sons in the light of day and handle them without gloves? *Get in* . . . and make sure you grab good hold of those boxes. Your wife has trekked all this way cradling them in her arms."

She hopped into the pickup with a single leap and slammed the door shut. I followed.

"Do you have the autopsy paperwork?" she asked.

I took it out of my backpack. She looked it over and handed it back.

"We're not going to prepare it here. Best do that at the Central Cemetery."

She twisted the key in the ignition and stepped on the accelerator, raising a cloud of dust. It was still daytime, but the moon was out: round like a bullet hole in the sky.

W here are we going to relocate all these people, Mayor?"

"You know the answer, Reyes: where we always do."

The chauffer probed no further. He was discreet. He knew just enough. And if he heard more than that, he kept it to himself. He did what he was told, nothing more, nothing less. Beneath his gray hair, weathered skin, and refrigerator dimensions, Reyes was a cautious man. He knew what to expect because he had assisted the five previous mayors, all of them appointed thanks to Abundio's string-pulling.

Escorted by that towering man, Aurelio Ortiz made his way through the waiting crowd. More than despise them, he feared them.

"Pick eighty numbers. . . . Everyone else can come back tomorrow. And when you finish, come upstairs, I need you for another matter."

The chauffer announced the instructions in a booming voice.

"Get your papers ready! The numbers are about to be called!"

Aurelio slumped into his office chair in front of a black computer screen. The powered-down monitor reflected the image of a man past his prime. The work he did at city hall was not respectable, but that was exactly the reason Abundio wanted him here.

When the plague broke out in the eastern mountains, Abundio diversified his interests. He no longer maintained ties solely with the irregulars, but also with human smugglers, who charged a fortune to those wanting to evade the border checkpoints. He did business with them all.

Making them believe they would be conveyed to a plantation, health post, or shelter, the smugglers abandoned dozens of men and women to their luck, letting them die of hunger and thirst. They extorted their victims two or three times the cost to transport them to where they could find work, usually on land that belonged to Abundio, who profited from those grim dealings.

Very few refugees made it across alive. The journey was long and arduous. The sun beat down on them during the day and at night the cold finished them off. They all looked leathery. Even if weak and sick, they kept on with their long trek, but most made it only as far as halfway before they collapsed, eventually buried by the wind and dust.

During winter, the water disinterred the bodies and carried them from the upper part of the river down to Tolvaneras. The government had to dredge the swamp of all the corpses mired there. That was why only plastic flowers adorned the graves. Any real flowers died from drought or deluge. Such was the paradox of that land: water, giver of life, could just as easily take it away.

Aurelio Ortiz was responsible for recruiting all the people. It made him feel guilty, and deep down he was. Barely forty, he already felt haggard. He grew up with no mother or siblings. He was the only child of the village teacher, a liberal with Alzheimer's who had decided he would await the end of the world reading Cervantes's interludes. When Aurelio departed for the provincial capital to study business administration and accounting, his father had already lost his mind. He returned two years later in a light suit, wielding a graphing calculator and a receipt book.

"Look, m'hijo, I know you didn't learn about numbers in Cundinamarca. But I didn't think you would betray the values I taught you."

"Listen, Papá. . . ."

"You listen to me!" he blurted, sitting upright in the hammock. "My only son and look what he turns into. Working for that corrupt thug Abundio and, on top of that, becoming his puppet at city hall! At this rate you'll end up like the Glass Lawyer—petrified that somebody will smash you into pieces!"

His father's lucidity came and went, punctuating the haze of childhood. In between, he left a trail of memories. Aurelio Ortiz wasn't sure who the lawyer his father had referenced was. He must have been a character from one of the books he read, which were of little interest to him.

"At this rate, not even tiny shards will remain!"

With his father's words still swirling around his head, he took his phone out of his pocket and punched in the number of Críspulo Miranda, the farmhand Abundio trusted with his animals.

"Críspulo? Mayor Aurelio Ortiz here." He gave a theatrical pause. "Get the dogs out. We're going to pay somebody a little visit."

Higinio and Salustio's lips were purple, and a gash cut across their chests: ten sutures, from top to bottom, just like the sutures that disfigured my abdomen, left to right. Visitación rubbed their cheeks with a cotton swab soaked in alcohol.

"Sing them something, so they won't forget your voice."

I looked at her as if she were crazy. And she was.

"You think they can't hear you?" she prodded, holding my gaze. "Sing, hum. Say something to them."

"I don't want to."

Outside, sunlight refracted off the crosses on the graves. A filthy, burnished peace had settled over them. Visitación kept rummaging around in a cupboard filled with jars and pots. She wouldn't stop pacing around the room.

"My father was a custodian at the Central Cemetery. When I was a girl, I was often sent there to bring him his meals, a coffee, or a glass of water." She turned around and kept talking uninhibitedly, which seemed to be how she did just about everything. "You know how people were buried back then?" I shook my head. "Straight in the ground. Nobody shrouded them or covered their faces. The soil fell directly onto them. . . ." She took Salustio into her arms and started rocking him. "Back then, the irregulars were the only ones who killed, guns blazing. *Bang, bang!*" she made a gun with her hand. "There was no respect or dignity. There's not any now either. . . ."

Her fingers covered by gloves, she rubbed Higinio's cheeks to dissolve the film of dust covering his face. She looked around, searching for something.

"Take the other little boy and dress him in that gown on the table." She indicated a crumple of white cloth.

"But it's a baptismal gown."

"Even better, that way he'll make his entrance up there looking fine."

The tunic smelled of dust. Even the cut looked old. I didn't want to dress either of my sons in such eerie attire. I wondered how many times the gown had been worn, who had worn it. What difference did it make, one way or another? Saying our goodbyes was enough.

"I would prefer it if they wore only their diapers."

"As you wish."

We returned the twins to their boxes, which Visitación had lined with white cloth to approximate little caskets.

"Take your time, I'll wait outside."

She closed the door carefully, leaving me alone with my sons.

I wanted to take them into my arms and press them tight against my body until I soaked them up. From the moment they were born, so much had come between us: the incubator, the neonatal nursery, the ICU. Now that I had them so close, I couldn't even bring myself to cuddle them.

Tears slipped down my cheeks. The more I brushed them away, the thicker and saltier they became. I didn't want to cry, not like this, as if I had simply accepted the way things were without demanding an explanation. I closed the boxes and exited the shed with them tucked beneath my arm. In the shade of a spiny holdback, Salveiro carved furrows in the sand with a stone.

Visitación wanted to help me, but I wouldn't let her.

"Get up, Talkalot. The time has come," she told my husband.

We piled into the pickup in silence, not looking at one another.

"Hold on tight to the boxes, Talkalot, the road's a bitch today!"

The wind was blowing hard, and the sunlight made the barbed wire gleam. After a long detour, we pulled onto a road full of potholes. There was nothing but thistles, sandpaper trees, and empty lots covered in trash that the goats browsed as if it were brush. We followed a deserted stretch of road. We weren't searching for a home or returning to a home we'd left; we were headed down the road toward a grave. Sometimes we came upon clapped-out cars and the horse-drawn carts that the scrap dealers used to ferry trash. The animals were so skinny you could count the ribs raised through their sorry skin.

Right at the detour toward the cemetery, a pickup truck with tinted windows veered toward us.

"This can't be good," said Visitación.

"How come?"

"No license plates. Around here, only Abundio operates like that."

"Who's he?"

Visitación clicked her teeth, her eyes glued to the rearview mirror.

"They're looking for me," she stated.

"Why?"

"This can't be good."

Stepping on the accelerator, she drove on without a word. When we reached the cemetery, we could hear dogs barking.

The mayor got out of the Mitsubishi. He wore linen trousers and a linen guayabera, all white, like an Easter treat. Críspulo Miranda leaned on one of the fences corralling the dog pen, waiting for him.

"Easy, Roco!" the overseer spat on the sand, yanking the leash. The animal sat on its hind legs.

"What's wrong with these brutes? Haven't you fed them?" Aurelio mopped his forehead with a white handkerchief.

"The hungrier they are, the worse they get."

"We just want to go give somebody a fright, that's all."

"Where?"

"Tolvaneras, there we'll find Visitación Salazar."

"In that case I'll take Azufre and Ánibal."

"Roco's enough."

"Last time, the old lady shot a gun over our heads. Best be prepared."

"Don't you argue with me, Críspulo." Aurelio put on his most commanding voice. The Indian snorted. "Go find Lucero and that other dog, the German shepherd Abundio brought here."

"I only take out the wolves."

"You'll bring out the ones I tell you to, dammit!"

The farmhand looked at him warily, then walked back to the pen.

Críspulo Miranda was not to be messed with. If he'd had a mother, he would have bartered her for two bottles of liquor. His hands were cut up, and his thumbnail filed like a claw. He was slim and tall, a man of few words. As a small boy everything had

been stolen from him, even his name. He had baptized himself
"Críspulo." Laborers had found him on the road to Mezquite,
huddled in a ditch cradling his father's head. The irregulars had
left him there after cutting his family to pieces.

The man grew up watching others die and be killed. It was his
nature. When he was brought to Alcides Abundio, the old man
took him in and entrusted him with simple tasks that needed no
oversight. Since at first he didn't talk at all, it was impossible to
know if he was deaf or an idiot. So, in the end, Abundio assigned
him just one job: feeding and otherwise minding the dogs that
guarded his property. Large, awful mutts, ferocious black beasts.
As well as feeding them, Críspulo trained and dewormed them. To
earn a little cash on the side, he neutered dogs. This was how he
started drinking, buying his liquor with the loose change from his
surgeries. He became as well-versed in aguardiente as he was in the
machete: the best on the border.

Críspulo got along with the brutes because he had been treated
like one. Nobody on Abundio's property handled those animals
with greater care and devotion. He groomed them morning and
night. He fed them, even taught them to hunt. From them he
learned the fundamentals: hunger, copulation, and defecation.
That was how he lived, divided between those three tasks.

He was somehow ageless, too old to seem juvenile, too simple
to be considered a mature adult. One day he was found stalking
a donkey with three German shepherds and two Dobermans. He
drove them closer, goading them with a rod. Enraged and raven-
ous, they pounced on the donkey, tearing into its hide. Críspulo's
expression didn't change, and he didn't call them off. Once the
dogs tore off its hide, Críspulo planted himself before the donkey
and started slashing it with the machete. The animal brayed so

much that the men and women who worked in the house hurried outside to see what the commotion was. They found him covered in blood, the machete still in his hand.

From that moment on, Críspulo recovered his voice and became old Abundio's shadow. He never left his side, day or night.

They were waiting at the cemetery entrance. Aurelio's eyes were shielded behind thick sunglasses and Críspulo stood reining in three leashed German shepherds. They were thickset animals, as fierce as lions.

Visitación climbed out of the pickup, a shovel in hand.

"Let me through, Indian. The couple with me are here to bury their babies." She looked Aurelio up and down. "Do you always dress so well to do Abundio's bidding, Mayor?"

"Show some respect, now. I've come in the name of the law."

"Abundio is not the law. He abuses, which is something else entirely."

Aurelio brought a hand to his face, which was covered in perspiration.

"You can't continue using this land." He dried his forehead with a handkerchief. "The cemetery is illegal, you know that."

"I don't need to explain myself to you, especially not now. Let me through."

Angustias grabbed the boxes from her husband, hopped out, and joined Visitación. Straggling, Salveiro caught up.

The biggest dog rose on its hind legs, baring its jagged teeth and black gums, and began to bark. The other two, riled up, growled.

"Respect the dead, Aurelio!" shouted Visitación. "And you too, Críspulo! Call off those animals!"

The farmhand slackened the leash, and the German shepherd jolted closer. Visitación swallowed. She was afraid, but Aurelio Ortiz was too.

"One more step, and I'll leave your head in a worse state

than your father's!" She lifted the shovel. "Don't make me! Out of my way!"

Críspulo was amused by all this. Aurelio still hadn't worked out whether his cruelty was innate or amplified by the half bottle of aguardiente he had drunk on the way here. After drinking, he behaved like one of his dogs.

The plan wasn't working, and the mayor knew it, but he stayed put, as if he were an innocent bystander. Angustias Romero strode forward and faced him, the boxes in hand.

"Let me through."

Aurelio adjusted his shades. Embarrassment, not the sun, blinded him.

"Let me through," she repeated, her voice steady, addressing Críspulo now.

"Angustias. Come here!" Salveiro tried to grab her arm.

"Let me go!" She shook him off.

"Let her go, Talkalot." Visitación lowered the shovel and waited, her hands on the grip.

A crooked smile crossed Críspulo's face.

"Nobody's stopping you, lady. You can walk right by, just try. . . ."

The chain, tight around its neck, had reopened an old wound on the German shepherd's scruff. Angustias marched toward the gate as though the men before her were a figment of her imagination, something she could will away with her pain. The German shepherd charged and leaped at her, but another yank from Críspulo stopped it short.

Angustias regarded him coolly, as if she were observing him from a distance. Without taking her eyes off him, she knelt in the sand, the boxes in her hands, and started crooning a lullaby often sung to children on the other side of the range.

Sleep, my child,
I have things to do,
Wash the diapers and prepare the food. . . .

Her voice struck Aurelio with the blunt force of her sorrow.
The mayor turned to Críspulo, who was gripping the chains with
his hook-nailed hands. The German shepherd cowered, folded its
hind legs, and hid its snout. It had caught a whiff of her pain.

Sleep, my child,
Sleep, my love,
Sleep, little piece of my heart.

The mayor wanted to tuck his tail between his legs and run
away from the man he had become.

Críspulo yanked on the leash again to whip up the animals, but
they wouldn't obey. They had become three more of the goats that
browsed the Tolvaneras garbage dump.

The farmhand returned the dogs to the Mitsubishi. He tied
them to the roll bar and waited, seating himself on the bumper.

Aurelio Ortiz approached Angustias, who raised her dust-
covered face and looked him in the eye.

"I just want to bury my boys."

The sand spun whirlwinds into the air. Still on her knees, she
gripped the boxes tighter and resumed her song.

Sleep, my child,
I have things to do,
Wash the diapers and prepare the food. . . .

Her voice was the only tree offering any shade.

heard my own voice as if it were another's. It left my lips pushed by the pebble of rage caught in my throat. I sang to dislodge it. The cemetery's sand covered my cheeks, forming a face mask cracked by tears. My eyes burned, as if I wept vinegar.

The longer my lungs emptied, the greater my rage: at the plague, at Salveiro, at God, and at these men who wouldn't let me pass. And even though the farmhand's dogs snarled in my face, I did not back down. It made no difference if they tore my lips to shreds. I would bite them right back to defend my sons. If these men were going to treat us like beasts, I would defend myself like one. I learned that on the road here. I shielded the boys with my body and plunged my face into the sand, out of fear, and out of a desire not to feel it ever again.

My voice was the cudgel. And the louder my song, the stronger my body grew to fight them. Everything had been taken from me, everything but my rage. If I could not pay for a grave, I was prepared to die for the sake of one.

That land was not mine, but it was land. I had grown used to it. On the roads we trekked until we reached the border, its soil caking my skin, as if somebody had buried me before my time. I would never become dust because I was already made of it.

My ears and throat hurt from holding in my sobs. When repressed, a scream inflicts damage. It's a bird slamming against the walls, looking for a window through which it might escape. Resurrected from his fevers, Salveiro lay his body over mine to protect me. I did not bother to push him aside. That was him: deadweight.

The man who said he was the mayor tried to take my hand—to offer me solace, apparently. I did not want his pity, I only wanted to bury my two sons. I don't remember how much time passed, or when the sun went down; I only know that, when I lifted my face, Visitación wiped my sand-encrusted lips with a handkerchief. The dogs were no longer there.

A gray cloud rolled in, presaging the storm. Visitación churned the wet mix in a hurry, hoping to beat the downpour. When she was ready, my husband grabbed Higinio's box, and I took Salustio's. We placed them into a chamber of cinder blocks right over the ground. Standing before the grave, I saw a life that could have been flash by.

Where would my children go when we sealed the tomb? Would they miss my scent? Would their gashes knit together in the dark? Would they be reborn in a place where I could find them? *Naive, Angustias, you were naive to believe they would live*, I thought.

Of the little hair I had left, I cut the tips of a few strands and placed them inside the grave. Just one would be enough for my boys to find their way back to this world. I would be waiting for them.

Visitación smoothed the wet mix with a trowel, all the while looking to the sky. She broke a branch off a spiny holdback to mark the grave. It was left to Salveiro to write their names in the fresh concrete, but he neglected to do it. So, in the end, I did.

The smell of wet earth spread through the cemetery, and the first drops fell heavy on the sand. We barely had time to take shelter in a shed heaped with wooden planks, mattocks, and shovels. The rain pelted down, washing away the reek of those men and their dogs, and erasing the letters just inscribed on our boys' grave.

Visitación let us spend the night. We had nowhere else to go.

"I'll be back tomorrow. Make sure to lock the door properly. Sometimes dubious types drop by."

She headed off toward Mezquite, her pickup's tires flinging mud from the puddles. Tolvaneras had become a quagmire, and my body ached more than the day I gave birth. But my journey, finally, had come to its end.

Lightning woke me. Salveiro's side of the sleeping mat was empty. I grabbed a machete hanging from the wall and went out after him. The whole place was still flooded, the full moon reflected in the puddles of muddy water.

"*Salveiro! Salveiro!*"

I looked for him in the lean-to; he wasn't there. Then in the toolshed; nothing. Beneath the spiny holdback; not there either. I found him kneeling before the boys' grave, a hammer in hand.

"What are you doing?"

Without turning, he landed a blow on the concrete, which was still setting. Only then did he turn, look at me defiantly, and strike again.

"I'm getting them out of here! You and that old woman want to take my sons away from me! Child snatchers!"

"You wanted to leave them at the morgue. If we'd done as you wished, they would have ended up in the trash."

"It's your fault they died! I told you! I told you we shouldn't leave, but you insisted!"

"They would have died if we'd stayed too."

"That's a lie! It's all your fault! You wanted them to die, so you wouldn't have to lug them around anymore!"

"Salveiro, you're sick, and you don't know what you're saying."

"I know you insisted on leaving, and that's why they're dead. . . ." He stopped, exhausted. "I have a right to choose where to bury them! They're still my sons!"

"Strike that again and I'll . . ."

He brought down the hammer once more.

"And you'll what? Hack me with the machete?" he scoffed.

I raised the blade.

"Drop the hammer!"

He landed another blow. And another.

"I have to get the boys out. You're not going to take them away from me!"

Another lightning bolt grazed the clouds with its white light.

"Salveiro, stop!"

I lowered the machete, but he kept landing hammer blows, sobbing like a child.

"You're as good as dead, Salveiro. And I won't be the one to bury you."

I turned on my heel and walked over to the shed, grabbed the backpack with his things, and left it outside. I locked the door and lay down on the sleeping mat, the machete still in hand. More lightning flashed across the dark sky. When the thunderclap sounded, my eyes were already closed.

For three days and nights I slept beneath the spiny holdbacks, a cluster of straggly shrubs. My body hurt, shattered by exhaustion. I drank water from the tap in the small shed and went back to the shade to lie down. I slept almost all day and kept my eyes shut even when I was awake.

The light was the only indication of how much time had passed since Salveiro left. On that last night I dreamed of him, waking up shouting and crying for my babies. Visitación was the one to wake me. I recognized her because of her colorful headscarf and the halo of wasps that accompanied her wherever she went.

"And Talkalot?"

"Gone."

There was silence.

"And what about you . . . when are you leaving?"

I didn't answer. I only wanted to sleep, to lay down beside my sons, to stay still until I took root like just another Tolvaneras tree. I wanted to be left in peace, to be switched off or unplugged like a lamp.

"Drink this, it'll get your blood moving." She handed me a mug of coffee. It was sickly sweet.

I found it hard to sit up, my body as heavy as a slab of concrete.

"You haven't eaten, have you? You've been here three days, and every one of those days I've found you asleep." She brought the mug to my lips. "Take a sip. . . . After you drink this, I'll take you into town."

"I want to stay here."

"Where? There's nowhere to stay. You have to get on with your life."

"I can work for you."

"I don't need help, and even if I did, I'd have no way to pay you," she snorted. "Besides, you know nothing of the dead. You aren't even strong enough to use a shovel."

"Yes, I am!"

The coffee was treacly and thick, very strong, sweetened with panela. I felt it sliding down my throat.

"I can do whatever you like, just let me stay."

"But there's nothing besides graves here."

"I don't care."

I had nothing left to say, but, unless she kicked me out of the cemetery herself, I would not budge.

"If you did stay, any work would be in exchange for a roof over your head and a bit of food at most."

"Where should I start?"

Visitación let out a loud laugh.

"You donkey! You stupid, silly woman. Your hunger's making you rave. . . . You don't know what you're saying! Look at your skinny arms! You don't even have the strength to dig a hole in the sand."

"I want to stay here."

"It's not so easy. You can't just snap your fingers and *presto* . . . it's done. First we need to make a few things clear." I nodded. "Here, the dead are sacred. We don't do anything that might disturb them, and we don't speak ill of them either. I return them to the earth, *respectfully*. I expect you to do the same."

I picked up the mug and took another sip of hot coffee.

"We're not mourners. We bury the bodies of others so they can rest in peace. . . ." Visitación peered into my eyes. "Why do you want to stay?"

"I want to be near my sons."

"That's it?"

"Why else would I want to?"

"I don't know. . . . You don't have any papers, maybe you have debts. Or your husband does."

I shook my head.

"I have two dead sons, that's all."

She studied me, looking for a sign: something to jump on, a reason to command me to leave. Without so much as a goodbye, she abruptly walked to the shed, took a look at the graves, and then climbed into the pickup. I didn't watch her leave. A deep weariness made me sink into the sand. I disintegrated like a clod of soil in the Tolvaneras breeze.

The next morning, Visitación returned with a pair of plastic boots.

"If you intend on staying, you'll need these," she placed them on the floor. "Do you have any questions?" She looked at me in silence. "If you have any questions . . ."

"Will the dogs be back?"

My sons didn't come back, and my womb withered. I dried out like a liana and put roots down in the sandy earth where my true loves slept, tucked inside two shoeboxes.

Visitación mostly ignored me. Occasionally, she asked me to do certain things, but nothing too complicated, nothing that might slow down her work. "Make some coffee, go get the shovel, cut these branches, go find some of these stones." Visitación aspirated her *s*'s and loaded stressed syllables with a whipcrack of authority.

She didn't keep a fixed schedule. Sometimes she came three or four times a day, other times she was away until the afternoon. Most often she showed up with the family of the deceased, less frequently, alone. It made no difference to me. It was enough that she let me live in the lean-to. Whenever for any reason she spent the night at Tolvaneras, I gave her the sleeping mat and slept in the hammock.

Visitación was incapable of passing unnoticed. She got down from the pickup showing off her shapely hips and strong legs. She off-loaded the bodies herself and spent hours preparing them for burial. She rarely stopped to rest. But when she did, she drank energizing powder mixes, took a few drags of her cigarette, then went back to work.

I survived on little. I ate what I could cook on the burner, and since there was tap water to drink and for making coffee, I didn't care about the rest. I went to great lengths to keep everything tidy, clean the graves, and carve out a niche for myself in the cemetery. If I wanted to earn the right to stay with my sons, I had to work.

The first few weeks, I churned cement until exhaustion over-came me. It was a way for me to mitigate my hatred for a God who killed us through hunger and amnesia. If Mezquite men drained their fury swinging their machetes, I did so with my hands. With them, I waged my own war, and beat back the demons that were gathering force inside and out.

I prepared loads of wet mix, churning it frequently so it wouldn't harden. If she needed it, Visitación filled a bucket with the cement and left, ignoring my greetings. When she tired of hauling concrete blocks and burying the dead, she smoked a ciga-rette near the wire fence, then went back to what she was doing.

"Do you need help?"

But she didn't respond, as if I were one more of her dead.

She reminded me of women from the eastern coast. She was helpful and flirty. She never untied her headscarf or went without those colorful leggings that accentuated her curves. And she was always accompanied by the wasps, a plague halo to coronate her in this kingdom of graves.

Whenever she spoke on the phone she shouted, as if, at the ends of the earth, volume improved coverage. She was quirky and moody. Sometimes she dealt with people brusquely; other times, she took forever to say goodbye, doling out well wishes and blessings.

"Don't go to the trouble, papi. I'll come to you," she would say, phone in hand.

She had a boyfriend who called her all the time. He worked at the Central Cemetery; I inferred as much because she asked him for every last detail of what went on there.

Once, she caught me spying on her.

"What are you looking at? Mind your own business! Go churn cement!"

That was how I spent my days, mixing mud with a stick and standing guard at the twins' grave. After repairing the damage wrought by Salveiro's hammer blows, I cleaned the headstone and planted a few seeds, so that my boys would at least have something living nearby. They never flowered.

I wasn't ready to leave, or to return to the eastern mountains. Nothing was there for me anymore. Here, at least, my past was at peace. Sometimes, in the distance, I heard the sound of dogs barking.

A man stepped out of a blue Chevrolet, said goodbye to the driver, and walked toward the gate. He had come alone, and that made me feel calmer, but I still didn't let him out of my sight. He didn't look like one of the mayor's lackeys, or a scrap dealer. He was young and wore shorts and sandals.

"Who are you?" I called out, shovel in hand.

"What was that?" He put his hand to his ear.

"Who are you? What do you want?"

"I'm Víctor Hugo. . . ."

Visitación left the shed swinging her hips.

"Papi . . . why aren't you at work? Wait a sec, I'll grab my things and we can get out of here."

"You're not going to introduce us?"

"This is Angustias. She's staying here while she finds a place. Isn't that right, m'hija?"

Víctor Hugo was waiting to be introduced as her boyfriend, but she ignored him.

"What are you doing, just standing there, Víctor Hugo? Come on, it's getting late!"

Before getting into the driver's seat, Visitación turned around.

"I'm off to Cucaña to buy some cement and return a few defective shovels. Víctor Hugo can't carry anything heavy because of his hernia, and I can't move all the bags alone. . . ."

"I'll help," I moved toward her.

She motioned to the pickup bed with her lips.

I climbed up in a flash and hung on next to the spare wheel, my back to the cabin. As soon as we took off, Víctor Hugo said something in a tiny voice I could barely make out. Visitación became furious.

"More money? You're not betting on cockfights again, are you?"

She slid the cabin window shut so I couldn't hear their conversation, but she was speaking so loudly that the glass between us did little. I pricked my ears. Víctor Hugo was murmuring, hunched over in the passenger seat. Each time he replied, Visitación's mood worsened.

"Look here, Víctor Hugo, I'm not stupid! You're hitting the town! I'm nobody's enabler. I don't hold back! I'm not lending you money, and I'm not letting you live at my place. I made that clear from the beginning. I want to be your mamita, not your mother!"

Víctor Hugo didn't open his mouth again until we reached Mezquite. He got out of the pickup still moping, but Visitación stuck to her guns.

"I've said what I had to say. And don't try to make amends. I'm in charge here, is that clear?"

"Visitación, reina, ditch him and come with me!" a young guy yelled at her from a motorbike.

"Careful or you'll lose your load, m'hijo. And have some respect, children should be seen and not heard!" She feigned offense, but deep down she loved the attention. Men's words made her feel beautiful.

He didn't see me, thankfully. I was unloading the empty drums. When I tried to carry both at once, one fell.

"Bring it over, Angustias, together we'll make short work of this." She turned to her boyfriend, emphatic. "And you run along to the cemetery, else the priest will come along and tell me I'm to blame for your idling!"

"You're not going to drop me off?"

"No, papi, you can walk. Your mamasota is busy, can't you see?"

Visitación adjusted her headscarf, hitched up her leggings, and began dragging the drum with both hands.

"Hurry up, Angustias! We have to go get cement after this!"

"What if I stay here to guard the bags, and afterward you take me to the cemetery?" Víctor Hugo tried another tactic.

"No, papito. I don't need you, at least not for this. Goodbye, my darling!" And she let out a laugh.

Aurelio Ortiz had never seen Abundio treat anybody the way he treated Críspulo. Nowadays he was the farmhand in charge of Abundio's dogs, his right hand when it came to the game fowl and other dealings on the hacienda, but it was only after many years that Abundio had started trusting him with these tasks. He had struggled to size him up, and once he did, he made the most of the donkey episode to keep him on a short leash.

Everybody knew the story, and relayed it sprinkled with exaggerated details. The devil had pushed him to do it; he had been possessed by the spirit of his decapitated father. "Bad boy," "Bad Christian," "The devil incarnate," they whispered behind his back. Críspulo was cruel, and Abundio liked that, but he was not sure where his loyalties lay. So, he decided to put him to the test.

"You never know, with Indians," he mused to his men when they told him what Críspulo had done with his machete. "With people like Críspulo, you need to make it clear who's boss, and whose side it pays to be on."

After returning from Sangre de Cristo, where he met with game-fowl breeders, guerrillas, and henchmen at his service, the old man dismissed Reyes and his bodyguards and searched the hacienda high and low for Críspulo. He found him in the shed. By that stage he was a young man, but his behavior remained bizarre and sullen.

Críspulo sat on his haunches, prying worms from the soil with a stick. He would probe them for a while, then drop them into his mouth still wriggling, slurping them down like muddy noodles. The old man, who had a gun slung over one shoulder, yanked him by the arm and, pressing the Winchester into him hard, escorted him into the house.

He had Críspulo rinse his mouth and seated him at the dining table. He made sure everybody saw. That way, he could insult his wife while he was at it; no doubt she would choose to go hungry upon discovering that the farmhand she found so repugnant had eaten off her plates. Who knew? With a little luck, maybe she would leave him once and for all, and be out of his sight forever.

Críspulo had never used a tablecloth, and he didn't know how to hold a fork. Until that day, he had always eaten in the dog pen, lifting grains of rice to his mouth with his fingers. Sometimes, out of pity, the other farmhands gave him a picadillo made from their leftovers, which he ate from the bowl like one of the German shepherds.

He grew up drinking directly from the pot of mazamorra, a lumpy corn brew full of weevils. He hadn't used a napkin before, much less tried arepas as white and soft as those Abundio had served. They were stuffed with white cheese and served with black beans, ground meat, and fried plantains.

"If you're hungry, eat," he said, motioning toward the plate.

Críspulo appeared suspicious and unsure. He grabbed the arepa with both hands and tore into it enthusiastically.

"Do you take good care of the dogs?"

Críspulo wolfed down the ball of cheese, butter, and flour. He felt it get caught and thumped his chest twice. He mopped up the black beans with the rest of the arepa and gulped it down without even a sip of water.

"I hear you know how to use a machete and treat my dogs like princesses."

The old man skewered a piece of fried plantain with the fork and moved it toward Críspulo's mouth, obliging him to try it. Críspulo chewed vigorously.

"Eat, eat up." Abundio's expression darkened. "I also hear you killed a donkey with a machete. Do you have anything to say about that?"

Críspulo stopped chewing.

"Don't pretend to be deaf and dumb with me, I know you can talk. . . ."

He gripped Críspulo's jaw.

"You killed my best beast of burden. . . ." He shoved the entire plantain into Críspulo's mouth. "Around here, I'm the only one who does any killing."

The boy coughed, choking.

"Swallow, you ungrateful fuck!" He shoved the fork even deeper. "I've treated you like a son, I've given you a roof over your head, food, a trade. And this is how you repay me, by butchering one of my beasts? *Eat, dammit!*"

Críspulo squirmed as he gagged.

"You're not getting up till you've finished."

He threw him down onto the table, pulling his pants down to his knees. Abundio's fly gaping, hands pinning his hips, he lunged at Críspulo, again and again.

"Learn! Learn! Learn!" With each shout, Abundio rammed him. Covered in dirt and semen, Críspulo whimpered, the plantain still lodged in his mouth.

When Abundio was done, he did up his fly and went out to the patio, his boots echoing in the quiet. In the dark, sprawled across the tabletop, Críspulo vomited a thick paste of half-chewed worms and beans. In the shed, the dogs barked, tied to the stump of a soursop tree.

n Mezquite, everybody was talking about Angustias Romero. Storekeepers referred to her as Visitación's assistant. They said she had lost her mind after losing her sons. According to them, this was the reason she had stayed on at Tolvaneras. Aurelio Ortiz wanted to know if it was true, so he went to where Angustias purchased gasoline once a week.

It wasn't hard to find her. She was using a hose to siphon fuel from the tank, which she would then clumsily spit out into a small plastic drum. When she noticed Aurelio Ortiz, she accidentally swallowed a mouthful and started coughing.

"What are you doing?"

She tried to push him aside, slapping him, but giddiness overcame her short temper. The mayor took hold of her and started hitting her on the back until she expelled reddish spittle on the sand.

"Stop, stop!" she straightened up.

Angustias Romero would not call a truce even when she was choking. Still disoriented, she seemed stronger, more hardheaded. When her coughing subsided, she looked around, alert.

"If you don't know how to siphon gas, why pretend to? You could have been poisoned!"

"Keep those dogs away, don't even think about bringing them any closer!"

Aurelio Ortiz snorted.

"There are no dogs here, just calm down."

He opened the pickup and threw her onto the seat. Little by little the color returned to her face, as did the icy gaze she shot him the last time they saw each other, back in Tolvaneras.

"Reyes, come here!"

The driver ambled over, his Glock in his belt.

"Keep your gun hidden, Reyes." The mayor lowered his voice. "Do me a favor: get in the lady's truck and follow me."

"I'm not going anywhere with you." Angustias coughed again.

"Shut it!" Aurelio chided. "And for once in your life, do as you're told!"

She was examined in the town dispensary without a fuss. Many in a sorrier state would die. This would pass with a big drink of milk.

"Nobody has died from swallowing a mouthful of gasoline." The doctor gave a harsh little smile. "At most you will have a touch of indigestion, maybe belch some fumes. So long as you don't smoke, you will be fully recovered in two days."

Angustias got up from the gurney, fixed her hair, and straightened up, as if she had swallowed a palm tree instead of gas.

"Angustias, wait," Aurelio tried to stop her, but she walked on without turning her head.

The mayor stood still, anchored to the spot on the clinic tiles, a handkerchief in hand. The giggles coming from the doctor and nurse snapped him out of his surprise.

"Good day, thank you for your time," he took his leave brusquely.

When he stepped out onto the street, Angustias had already driven off. She had snatched the keys from Reyes and left, furious. He tried to catch her, but it was too late. She had already turned right at the main street, at full speed, headed for the interstate.

"Don Aurelio . . ."

"What is it, Reyes?"

"Should I take you home, so you can get changed?" The driver looked him up and down.

His pants were stained with mud and gasoline. Aurelio snorted, feeling ridiculous beneath the diabolical midday sun.

Jairo Domínguez claimed to know every town in the mountains. Of the twenty-five, he had resided in twenty-four. He traveled from one to the other, playing the accordion his German grandfather left to him, enlivening so many of the fiestas and wakes held from Sangre de Cristo southward.

What providence hadn't bestowed upon him in riches, it had made up for with his ear and way with words. He was tall, a mestizo with fair hair. He had large green eyes, two points of light fitted like emeralds into a cinnamon face. He liked to drink and knew by heart all the songs from the mountains, and some from the coast too. Wherever he went, he improvised corridos, joropos, and cumbias, singing of infidelities, liaisons, and any dirty laundry he could find. Not even Abundio was spared the black humor of his verses. He called him "the gun-toter." The old man liked the moniker, and for that reason never had a bullet put in the clown.

According to what Jairo told friends and strangers, his father's father had come to the western mountains from Berlin, fleeing a war nobody had heard of. Nobody in Mezquite thought this added up. "Jairo, *German?* But his name is more criollo than jute and his skin more coppery than mud!"

It made no difference to him whether they believed him or not. He only cared for his songs. Everyone in Mezquite knew them, not because they liked his music, but because they wanted to discover whether an event from their own lives had found its way into one.

The townspeople gathered for him at an establishment in the

market where a slim and pale Lebanese man reigned, serving coffees and liquor from the other side of a long bar. It was a dark cantina the singer frequented to eat sponge cake bathed in ponche, a beverage made of coffee, sugar, cinnamon, and aguardiente. Anybody who wanted to know the ins and outs of others' lives treated him to another round of whatever he was drinking in a sort of patronage conferred by the cowardly and spiteful.

I met him soon after I arrived in Mezquite, at the first wake Visitación took me to. The following day, once everybody had finished exchanging farewells, we would bury the deceased at Tolvaneras.

Jairo arrived at the widow's house with some water.

"Drink, woman . . . so the dead man doesn't reach the other side with a dry mouth!"

He moved the large clay vessel over to the casket, which the family had propped up against the wall of a house constructed from concrete blocks. Inside the casket lay the body of a man dressed in a darned suit, his head wrapped in cloth. He had been mutilated by a machete.

"I'm doing this because you're my comadre," said Visitación to the widow, who embraced her between sobs.

"You're a saint, you are. *A saint!*"

"Let me go, woman," she grunted, annoyed. "I don't like these wakes with music and revelry, they never end well."

It was true. Usually, they ended with machete slashes.

"Your husband was a good man, Ramona, but the drink led him straight to the grave," she frowned, serious. "Do me a favor and keep all these people under control."

The widow wallowed in her sobs even more, against Visitación's advice. Visitación turned to give me instructions.

"You stick with me, and no taking even a sip of liquor."

She sat by the door and waited, not opening her mouth, until the first mystery of the rosary began.

The heat was suffocating, and the sun beat down on the guests: men and women drawn here more out of hunger than grief. At wakes in all towns in the western mountains, chicken broth, boiled yucca, and alcohol were offered in abundance. Sometimes friends of the dead man, storekeepers too, donated salted fish or dried meat. They did so out of pity or remorse.

The dead man's sisters led the prayer. After completing six mysteries of the rosary, they picked out a few litanies, which the guests followed with their mechanical responses:

> *Holy Mary,*
> *pray for us.*
> *Mother of God,*
> *pray for us.*
> *Holy Virgin of Virgins,*
> *pray for us.*
> *Mother of Christ,*
> *pray for us.*
> *Mother of the Church,*
> *pray for us.*
> *Mother of divine grace,*
> *pray for us.*
> *Mother most pure,*
> *pray for us.*
> *Mother most chaste,*
> *pray for us. . . .*

By the patio, three boys were chasing an iguana that had fallen out of a tree. I saw it happen. Its body when it landed made a sound like a rock encased in rubber. The boys were quicker than the lizard and pounced on it, pulling at it. After hog-tying it with cotton yarn, they crouched down.

They poked it with a stick several times. The animal twisted away, nervous. They jabbed its scaly belly and combed its crest, top to bottom, with fine sticks that sounded like fencing foils being whipped in the air. One of the boys wanted to poke a stick through the iguana's belly, but the eldest pushed him away, knocking him to the floor.

"Don't touch it! I saw it first!" he challenged the others.

Holding a long rod in both hands as if it were a sword, he plunged the tip into one of the animal's eyes, then into the other. He bored them unhurriedly, until the sockets were empty. The boys, excited by the blood, thronged the body of the iguana, while the women kept praying in the entranceway.

Mother inviolate,
pray for us.
Mother undefiled,
pray for us.
Mother most amiable,
pray for us.
Mother most admirable,
pray for us.
Mother of good counsel,
pray for us.
Mother of our Creator,
pray for us.
Mother of our Savior,
pray for us. . . .

The boy grabbed the blind iguana by the head and shook it in the air. It was his; it had been his idea to knock it down with stones and tie it up afterward. He could do whatever he liked with it, and that was what he demonstrated when he stuck thorns into its belly, pressing the barbs with the tip of his shoe.

The others tried to pull it away from him. It wasn't fair, they wanted their turn, but the eldest defended his right with kicks and clobbered the reptile against the ground as if it were a sneaker. "It's mine! It's mine!"

> *Virgin most prudent,*
> *pray for us.*
> *Singular vessel of devotion,*
> *pray for us.*
> *Mystical rose,*
> *pray for us.*
> *Tower of David,*
> *pray for us.*
> *Tower of ivory,*
> *pray for us.*
> *House of gold,*
> *pray for us.*
> *Ark of the covenant,*
> *pray for us. . . .*

I went over without making my presence felt, trying to understand what they were saying. What remained of the iguana was writhing in death throes. The boy snatched it violently and squeezed it like a lemon. The more pressure he exerted, the more the lizard flailed, distraught from the via crucis and the punctures.

All of them wanted to participate. They had helped hog-tie it too, they had a right, but they only got to watch. None of them dared contest their leader. They hated him for it, though their grievance preceded this incident. Maybe they would not be rid of their resentment until they could kill their own iguanas.

> Gate of heaven,
> pray for us.
> Morning star,
> pray for us.
> Health of the sick,
> pray for us.
> Refuge of sinners,
> pray for us.
> Comfort of the afflicted,
> pray for us.
> Help of Christians,
> pray for us. . . .

The animal stopped moving its legs. Triumphant, the boy showed off the iguana body before throwing it at the feet of his deflated companions. He turned around and climbed the mango tree, where he could watch over the patio. Vultures flew over, their black feathers spiraling to the sandy ground. I went back inside the house to where the prayers were being intoned. The other boys followed me, humiliated and robbed of their right to kill, stewing in their rage and shame.

When the novenary finished, the men got out of the hammocks they'd been dozing in and convened to play dominoes. The dead man's sisters opened the vessel of water by the casket. Then the coplero played his first notes on the accordion. He played and sang several songs without stopping. Some he invented, others were by request. No sooner had one finished than another began. Between songs he took swigs of caña blanca.

After retreating to a table by a tree, the players slammed down the tiles and improvised rhyming phrases, providing commentary on their own moves. "The boxcars, take that!" "Tigers don't eat tigers!" "Blocked!" shouted the winners to wrap up the game. Then they flipped over the tiles, shuffled them about with both hands, and started over.

The observers took long swigs from their bottles as they collected the bets. Those who drank at first cried later, and vice versa. Others tossed back their drinks and improvised justas that the coplero accompanied on the accordion and with two maracas made from calabash gourds. Removed from the rest, a group of mourners stood near the casket, listening to Visitación give an account of the Old Testament.

"'Call unto me, and I will answer thee, and shew thee great and mighty things, which thou knowest not.' That's what verse three of the prophet says," she read in a serious, theatrical affect.

The women looked at her, crossing themselves.

"Be wise, Ramona! And listen carefully to the chosen ones . . . ! Learn from Jeremiah, who drank from the chalice of pain," she finished, her hands held high.

Around us, people were whiling away the night with bottles of aguardiente, coplas, and a shove or two between those who had drunk too much. With little to go before daybreak, the widow kneeled before the casket and, turning the palms of her hands to the sky, raised her voice, rousing everyone with her cries.

"He's drunk all the water, Jairo! He's drunk it all! He can go, now!"

The coplero paid no mind to the woman, or to the crowd of

freeloaders and rubbernecks jostling for a better view of the empty vessel. If, after an entire night, the heat had desiccated the vessel, the aguardiente had done the same to everyone's brains. By that stage, they were all exhausted from so much crying and dancing together.

"The dead man is leaving! The dead man is leaving!" they chanted.

"One more song, Jairo! One more, to send him off!" they shouted, gathering in a circle near the wooden box.

People who lived in Mezquite chose to believe in desperate miracles. What difference did it make to have faith in one thing or another? They drank themselves silly not out of grief, but out of relief to find themselves still alive. The coplero grabbed a bottle of aguardiente, took a swig, and spat on the floor. Then he let the rest of the alcohol trickle out until it formed a cross on the sand.

Visitación and I stayed on our feet, holding our ropes and shovels, ready to take the deceased away. We looked at Jairo guiding the fiesta. Then I felt that a glass bell rose above us.

saw Jairo again two weeks later, at the Cucaña market. Surrounded by bread and fish stalls, he was singing the story of a woman turned to salt by the wind.

Everybody tells her lies,
she is grieving too many goodbyes.
She crossed the mountains penniless,
nursing her sorrow in the darkness.
She ran at the gun-toter's dogs with a refrain,
and, banished from the world of the living,
among the dead decided to remain.

When I showed my face, wanting to hear better, Jairo stopped playing his accordion, greeted me with a tip of his red cap, and resumed:

She came from Sangre de Cristo
and ended up in Tolvaneras.
I, who have my wits about me,
if I sing that I saw her in Mezquite,
that's because I truly did, you see.

None in the crowd recognized me, but all the same I felt embarrassed. I hurried away, passing counters heaped with chickens, their throats slit, and ice-covered fish on metal trays.

I went to the cooperative to collect some gasoline and the week's drinking water. Crossing near the truck lot, I searched for the girl who had given me Visitación's phone number. I couldn't find her. All the girls her age looked alike: nothing but skin and bones. They went hungry more often than the boys and mothers put together. It was sad to see them trying to make ends meet, bald and starving.

"How many more drums do you need loaded up?" When I spun round, there was Jairo. He still had his accordion strapped to his chest. "Are you going to Tolvaneras?"

I nodded.

"I'm headed to a place nearby. Drop me off and I'll help unload your gasoline."

"Some other day, Jairo."

The cooperative worker helped move the drums with a hand trolley, then sat them in the bed of the pickup.

"How about a drink?"

"I don't drink."

"But I do."

"I don't have any money."

"My treat," he laughed, making his accordion sound. "Come on! All day on the go, hauling one thing after another. . . . Treat yourself."

We stepped inside a cheap restaurant. Jairo chose the end table.

"The bar would be better, I'm in a rush."

From there I had a view of everything.

"You're a strange lady," he muttered.

The first round of truckers had left the market, and the women were queueing outside the restroom so they could clean themselves up and redistribute their money. There were noticeably more than last time.

"What are you looking at?" he asked.

"None of your business."

"Ah, I know! A lot of your compatriots can be found around here, right?"

"Uh-huh," I nodded.

"They're all prostitutes."

"I'd best be leaving, I've got a lot to do. . . ."

"Wait, Angustias!" he grabbed my arm. "*Alright, alright!* I'll shut it. I won't mention that again, just stay for a bit."

I sat back down on the stool, not wanting to make a scene.

"Bartender, pour me a beer!" he cried. "As for the lady . . . what would you like, Angustias?"

"Water."

"That's it?"

"I want water, Jairo."

"Well then, water . . ."

The server, a mixed-race man with a coastal accent, glanced at me, and then at Jairo, who coughed and dismissed him.

"Do you like the song I composed for you?"

"Which one?"

"The salt one . . ."

"Was it for me?"

"Who else would it be for?"

Outside the sellers traded fruits, vegetables, fish, and beef sirloin that stained the butchers' aprons. The heat was not oppressive yet, but it was headed for it. Jairo's forehead was damp. His body emitted a sharp perfume of sweat and aguardiente. Up close, he looked younger than I had thought.

"Aren't you too old to be surviving by working gigs? Didn't your mother ever tell you to get a proper job?"

"My mother is dead," he answered.

"My apologies, I didn't know."

"Don't sweat it, it was a long time ago."

"But, is this how you earn a living?"

He looked at me, surprised.

"What do you mean, 'this'?"

"Making up songs."

"I don't make them up, I compose them. And yes, it's how I make a living. I get a call to come to one town or another. I go, I sing, and I get paid. If I'm lucky I might even get a call from abroad one of these days. Or somebody will put a video of me on the internet, and I'll be famous."

The barman served a beer and glass of water.

"Thanks, man." Jairo wiped the mouth of the bottle with the palm of his hand and took a swallow.

"And the story about your grandfather being German, is it true?"

"That's what my mother used to say. She said it so often that people believed her."

"And what does your father think about you bumming around making a living off your accordion?"

"I don't know him. He left my mother before I was born." He took another swig. "You don't want to try the water, Angustias?"

I sipped, not thirsty, to pass the time.

"Are you married?"

I nodded.

"And your husband . . ."

"He's sick now."

"And you're not taking care of him?"

"He needs to take care of himself, I have to work." I looked at the clock. "Thank you for the water."

"Hey, don't go. . . ."

I made my way toward the pickup. The women were flitting from trailer to trailer. At this hour business was slow. So, they reapplied their lipstick and smoothed their shorn hair while hoping for a trucker or two to save the day.

I climbed into the cabin and adjusted the mirrors. Before leaving, I saw Jairo in the reflection. He waved from the doorway of the bar. His skin shone in the sun.

Visitación left the motor idling and marched over to the tool-shed. She returned with several ropes and the axe we used to cut wood into boards for the caskets.

"Where are you going?" I asked, a shovel in hand.

"To Cuchillo Blanco."

"I'm coming with you."

"This is serious business, Angustias."

"Do you see me laughing?"

She shrugged her shoulders.

"Get in, then."

Forty miles lay between Tolvaneras and Cuchillo Blanco, the oldest of several hamlets bordering the eastern mountains' cane and tobacco plantations. Its name referenced both the inevitable reality that all celebrations there ended in knife fights, and its aguardi-ente, the purest in the region. One little glass was enough to set the heads of an entire regiment on fire. Storekeepers handed it out in small bottles nestled in brown paper bags.

Almost all Cuchillo Blanco's inhabitants were women, most of them tobacco pressers. Business had dwindled over time, but there was still work to be had. Several generations had grown old kneel-ing before stacks of dry leaves while their husbands and sons spent their days swinging machetes, harvesting cane. Even women who worked in the border cities came back on their days off to collect cane and press tobacco, work that fed their families.

That was how people in the area lived, until Abundio bought up the plantations. In his hands, the whole operation collapsed. The men stopped working in the fields, instead becoming sicarios or runners. Sometimes not even that. Mothers and grandmothers kept scorching their knuckles and fingertips to bring home money. Their daughters and granddaughters fared no better: they ended up on the border, selling contraband or collecting tolls from truckers crossing the interstate bridge.

The men who kept out of the brawls and benders of Cuchillo Blanco drank in the doorways of their homes, mangy edifices blighted by missing tiles and broken windows. They resembled veterans of an invisible war. Easily recognizable, they were absent an ear, nose, or some other extremity, and reeked of sweat and alcohol. If they lived, it was penance for their sins in this land.

The youngest drove around in their trucks, the music cranked up. They spent more time at cockfights than looking for work. The drug trade provided them with a living, and that was more than enough.

At number 3 on Calle Ezequiel stood the skeleton of a building that once had stucco on its balconies and plants in its gardens. The windows of the large house were shuttered with wooden boards. As for the doors, with their dried-out, split timber, they had their locks missing, some marked with black crosses left by irregulars to record their movement through the towns.

Several neighbors stood waiting for us outside the gate.

"What a relief you're here! The Frenchman's house smells like death, and it's been days since he set foot outside." An old lady with coppery skin and black hair would not stop crossing herself.

Visitación took hold of a handkerchief she had tucked into her waistband, covering her nose with it, and tied the ends behind her head. Then, she grabbed the axe and ropes while I pushed the cart with both hands. We climbed a few wooden steps that had no handrail. The whole place reeked of rot, and the heat was hellish.

"Here we are." Visitación came to a stop before a wooden door.

She swung the axe and delivered a blow, but only a few splinters went flying. She raised her arms again and brought down the axe twice more, until the door caved. Hanging from the roof, the body of a man swayed like a bell clapper. A cloud of glossy flies wheeled around his face, their larvae devouring his eyes. At his feet, a colony of maggots teemed like a living, repulsive cream.

"Ay, Frenchman, my dear!"

Visitación made her way inside the room, which was bare of furniture, and examined the body for a few minutes. An erection was swelling the man's fly. His violet tongue was lolling as if a scream had dried up in his throat. He was as stiff as a peg. I moved closer to help her, but she told me to step back.

"Nora, get up here!" she ordered the neighbor.

The woman shouted something from the lower floor. I couldn't make it out.

"Get up here, you cowardly old bag!" retorted Visitación. "She asks me to come, and then doesn't help! Come here!"

The elderly woman appeared in the doorway. She dragged her feet as she neared, making the sign of the cross over and over.

"Don't make me come in there, Visitación. It's the work of the devil!"

The man was still swinging like a pendulum, an exclamation point dangling from the roof.

n Cuchillo Blanco, Jacques Thierry was known as the Frenchman. He was a missionary who arrived in town alongside Lidia, a tall, dark young woman, with sturdy legs and a thick waist. Pushing fifty, he was a blond white man. The townspeople pretended to buy the story that he and Lidia were family, but behind closed doors they proposed more interesting theories.

The Frenchman had met Lidia in a prison in Switzerland, where she was serving time for drug trafficking. She had been caught with a stomach full of cocaine capsules after being intercepted on a flight from Amsterdam. Jacques visited her while she served out her sentence, and when she was set free, he took her to work on a farm.

Lidia, who was born in a starved town in the western mountains, was far from content in that cold, boring place. She wanted to see her mother and daughters again, even though they had disowned her after her arrest at the airport was splashed across the papers. She convinced the Frenchman to pack his few belongings and cross the sea. Who knew? Maybe, with a little luck, he would end up liking the hamlet she had left behind when she was misled by a lamentable character. He had left her stranded with the drugs, not even paying for her lawyer.

They arrived in the town with four bags between them. They found the family home deserted and looted. Not a soul wandered the streets, and the abandoned businesses were falling to pieces. The irregulars had got there first, and they had carted everything off. There was no trace of Lidia's parents and sisters either. The land had swallowed them up. They waited at a bus stop, took the first bus that passed by, and decided to get off in Cuchillo Blanco.

The Frenchman fell in love with the mountains. With their freezing nights and dry afternoons. With their burning sun like a sour orange, and their hot wind, which made his lips flake. He wasn't sure how they would earn a living, but he proposed to Lidia that they start over here. He established a community center where he delivered basic medical care, spread the gospel, and taught reading and writing. Lidia started making trips in a truck they bought in installments with credit from Caja Rural. She worked as a mover and transported goods to the Cucaña market. She would return with little, the remainders of whatever she managed to sell. He attended to the townspeople free of charge, but the neighbors returned the favor by taking him eggs, coffee, and the vegetables they grew on their small farms.

Things were good for three years, until the irregulars detained Lidia at a roadblock. She refused to hand over the truck keys. They dragged her from the steering wheel amid rifle-butt blows, but even then she wouldn't give up the keys. After setting the truck on fire, they kidnapped her. If the Frenchman wanted to see her again, he would have to pay an exorbitant ransom that he could not have raised in ten years.

They gave him two weeks.

The Frenchman sold everything: his case of medical equipment, the furniture, his watch, and even the stove, but it was not enough. Frantic, he went to Tolvaneras to beg for Visitación's help. Thanks to her and some neighbors' pity, he secured part of the money. When he went to hand it over at the meeting spot, the guerrillas refused. Half was missing.

"It's the full sum or nothing!" demanded a man in fatigues.

The next morning, a group of children found Lidia's body floating facedown in the Cumboto. Alerted by the day laborers, Visitación collected the body after the police had done their work and told Jacques the news. From then on, he stopped going out, sealing his windows with planks ripped from the roof and shutting himself in to drink. If the world kept turning outside, it was only to remind him that he would never again see Lidia.

"He hanged himself . . . out of grief," Visitación pressed a hand to her forehead and sighed. "May the Lord bless you and keep you, Frenchman."

The forensics team took three hours to arrive. It was comprised of two large men with caña blanca on their breath. They stepped through the doorway accompanied by a police officer, measured the body, and snapped some photos while the officer took a statement from the elderly woman, the one who had made the sign of the cross. After cutting him down, they covered him in a sheet and heaved him onto a metal gurney.

The Cuchillo Blanco morgue occupied three floors of a concrete building surrounded by fried-snack stalls and hearses. They were parked next to the dumpsters and the police cruisers. Hawkers went in and out without oversight, and some even sold drinks in the corridors.

On the lower floor, huddled in a windowless room, a dozen men and women waited their turn to collect the bodies of family that had been taken by surprise when the Cumboto flooded as they tried to cross it illegally. Only the ones who knew how to swim managed to save themselves. Fishermen who combed the waters for peacock bass and trout alerted the police. The swollen bodies were entangled in their nets. And despite police boats patrolling the river all the way to its mouth, many bodies disappeared, spirited away by the strong current.

Unaffected by the tragedy, or maybe neck-deep in it, a group of children was making a racket. They argued, pushing and shoving one another. A girl who was a little older separated them, but not for long. The mother and father of the boys, completely spent, were fast asleep, hugging their backpacks.

"Stop it already, or I'll report you to your parents!" she yelled.

"The word's not *report*, stupid. It's *tattle*."

"Keep still! Behave yourself!" She tried to grab him by the arm, but he wriggled away.

"My parents won't listen to you! They're asleep because my uncle died!"

"I don't care—when they wake, I'll tell them everything you've done."

"You're not my mother, you're not the boss of me! My uncle drowned, and it's your fault!"

"Shut your face!"

"Witch, witch! You're a witch!" the brat persisted.

I drew closer to make out the girl's face. It was her—*the girl from Cucaña!* She seemed just as bossy but tired: now she wore a defeated expression. She had lost weight, her hair now short. Her bangs and the ends at the nape of her neck had been poorly cut. She sported faded shorts and a white shirt.

"Have some respect and quit your shouting. You're not supposed to talk about the dead," she admonished.

"I talk about whoever I want. Don't boss me, scumbag!"

She grabbed him by the arm and shook him, but the kid started punching her in the stomach.

"When my parents wake up, I'm going to tell them you're dirty. It's your fault my uncle drowned. He only liked you slipping your hands under the blanket. I saw you! Showing off in those tight clothes of yours, like Papá says!"

The girl swiveled and marched with her shoulders hunched over to a plastic chair on the other side of the waiting room. I had a little something in my pocket. I had bought it that morning to decorate my boys' grave. It was a clay bird, one that emits a trill when you fill it with water and blow. I went over to her.

"Don't mind him."

She raised her eyes. Her eyelids were swollen and her cheeks flushed.

"Blow." I handed her the whistle.

She warily took the little figurine, put her lips to it, and blew hard until a birdsong warbled. She looked at me in astonishment. And blew again.

"Could I borrow this?"

"It's a gift."

Her round eyes fixed on mine.

"I didn't see you at Cucaña again. Where did you go?"

"Did you find Visitación?" she asked, the whistle between her hands.

I nodded.

"Tuck it away. When you're annoyed or sad, blow it."

She admired the clay bird without saying a thing.

"Consuelo, come here!" somebody shouted from the hallway.

"What a lovely name. You never told me . . ."

"I know yours. You're Angustias."

They called her again.

"Your family wants you."

"They're not my family," she retorted sullenly.

"You're too big for this, but it's all I have," I motioned toward the whistle. "If you take care of it, it will take care of you."

She didn't seem all that convinced.

"Will it die too?"

"If you make it a nest from newspaper, no."

"Are you sure?"

"I promise."

We didn't stop, not even to refuel. The light faded as we drove, as if the sky were being wrung out, until the last ray was gone. Visitación opened the glove box, pulling out a small cigar wrapped in cellophane. She tore the plastic with her teeth, placed the cigar between her lips, and lit it with the car lighter. She took a puff, exhaling three rings of white smoke, and offered it to me.

I tried it. I had a coughing fit.

"You don't know how to smooooke!"

We laughed as the gray pickup kept on toward Tolvaneras.

"How long have you been doing this?"

"Smoking?"

"No, burying people."

"All my life! When I was seven, I was already watching burials. My old man would arrive at the cemetery at five in the morning and spend the whole day there. I started by taking him rice and chicken for lunch. While I waited for him to finish eating, I would lend a hand at the small morgue next door. I cleaned the equipment, swept, mopped. The morticians explained what each of the instruments was for."

She leaned forward over the steering wheel, as though she were giving a speech. I handed her the cigar and settled back in the seat. The night turned cold, and the breeze brought with it the scent of bushy lippia, a plant that flowered at the foot of moriche palms and around swamps.

"At fifteen, I performed my first necropsy." Visitación used technical terminology to puff herself up. "That time I was given a beating." She let out a laugh. "Somebody had to do it. It made things happen for me. There were almost no morticians, and I was young, but I was ready and willing."

She swerved to avoid a goat on the stretch of road, then resumed.

"Once I had to perform an autopsy on a man killed in a machete fight in Cocito, but somebody went and told my mother: 'Your daughter's off hacking up a dead body.'" She imitated the neighbor's scandalized tone.

I wound up the window and peered out at the hills, wondering where Salveiro would be, or whether he had died on one of the paths.

"My old lady came down to the cemetery and waited." My focus was pulled back to the conversation. I was no longer exactly sure what Visitación was talking about. "When I came out, still wearing a mask, she exploded. 'Ay, what a disgrace! What do you think you're doing? Just you wait until I see you at home.' When I stepped through the door, she snapped a broom handle over my head." Visitación took a handkerchief out of her pocket and mopped her forehead. "She wasn't being mean; she was scared I might catch a disease." She took another puff of her cigar, illuminating the dark with its red circle. "The day my mother died, I opened her up without shedding a tear. . . . 'Mother, if you gave birth to me, and made me as strong as I am, then why should somebody else prepare you for the grave? Why should a stranger be the one to make you look beautiful?'" She exhaled cigar smoke and continued. "I didn't want anybody going up to her casket thinking the mortician had left one nostril of her nose more open than the other. 'As for the dress you'll wear, I'll make sure it sits just so.' That's what I would tell her when she was alive, and back then she would respond, 'You're crazy. I only hope God will let me watch over you after I'm dead.

You'll end up in an asylum.'" Visitación let out a booming laugh. "I was the first woman in Mezquite to become a mortuary assistant! They even sent me to the capital to study! Back then people were ignorant and invented strange stories. They said pregnant women couldn't touch dead bodies, but I have a daughter who by a matter of minutes wasn't born in the morgue. I would start the year giving birth and end it pregnant!"

"How many children do you have?"

"Four! Two girls, grown women now, but they left town. They were right to. This land will only make them bitter. Two boys too, but they died. One after getting tangled up in drugs, the other after getting involved with a married woman."

"And your husband?"

"After twenty-six years, he accused me of loving the dead more than him. 'If you make me choose between you and my dead . . . ,' I told him, 'I'll take my dead because what you give me, anybody can.' He was a bit like your husband, Talkalot. Only half a man."

It didn't matter if what she said was true. Visitación pronounced each word as though it had been inscribed on a tablet, and that was enough. Her life story was like an Our Father—a truth without explanation.

"I don't need a husband. Everybody loves me! Visitación is better known than the Virgin Mary!"

She wasn't wrong. As we toured towns across the region, people sought her out, calling her by her given name. They went to her for solace and to bury their dead. She always listened attentively.

"I sculpt any face. When I started, I worked on faces disfigured by landmines. The irregulars still use them. It took eight or ten hours to prepare a body. Then I was forced into retirement. So, I got involved at Tolvaneras and started my own graveyard. Finally,

I had the freedom to do what I wanted with my dead. I cleansed them and dressed them."

"If you were retired, how did you get clearance?"

"I don't need papers. God's approval is enough for me."

She took a final drag on her cigar and pitched it out the window. I watched it sail away and flare in the wind, until it disappeared without a trace into the night.

On the first anniversary of my sons' deaths, I rose early. I made coffee and collected loose flowers to decorate their grave. When I arrived to lay them there, I found two wooden sculptures of jaguars, one for each boy. The figures were carved out of branches. I inspected the other graves one by one but found nothing else. They had been placed there purposefully.

Visitación tooted the horn several times.

"Angustias! Are you coming or not?"

"Wait!"

"Get a wriggle on, woman!"

I grabbed the jaguars and jumped into the pickup. We had to get to Puerta Grande jail before eight.

Once a month, Visitación Salazar visited a penitentiary 120 miles from Mezquite, the only one large enough to house prisoners from both the eastern and western mountains. It served as a detention center for people waiting to be deported. The prison was divided into a north wing, for men, and a south wing, which accommodated around fifty female inmates crammed inside. Visitación instructed them in Bible readings, an activity that pleased the prison authorities because it did not involve wielding tools, so additional surveillance was not required.

Only well-behaved women who had applied for probation or those serving for minor offenses could attend the workshop. Teaching those women, Visitación distracted them not only from the poverty they would encounter when they left the penitentiary, but also from the loneliness they were already suffering between those prison walls. At least the dead we buried had a place to rest. These women did not have that.

In contrast to the men in the north wing, who could see their wives, lovers, or children, nobody visited these women. Not even their mothers, if they had them. Not husbands, children, or siblings either. They had been erased from their loved ones' lives; nobody wanted to know anything about them. If one of the women made a request to receive visitors, she would have to wait months unless she sped up the process by sleeping with the prison officers, men who oversaw the female guards and raped the inmates without even bothering to blackmail them first.

In those monthly two-hour sessions, Visitación performed the sacred scriptures. So she said grandiosely. The psalms and verses were of little import; what she really intended was to teach them to read. In time, and after quite a bit of paperwork, she gained permission to teach them to carve mesquite, a good wood for making crosses and boards, not only firewood.

They almost always recreated *The Last Supper* or images of the Virgin and the sacred heart, some with more defects than others, which Visitación sold in Cucaña. With the money she made she bought baguettes, sanitary napkins, and cigarette packs; newspapers too, and notebooks and pencils. At the prison gate, the female guards often confiscated the cigarettes and sanitary napkins for their own use.

Only a few inmates met the requirements to participate. Visitación knew them all: Marcela, who had completed the sixth year of her manslaughter sentence—she killed her partner when he tried to murder her with a bat. Then there was Sonia, put away for drug trafficking; Lorca, a woman reported by her ex-husband for desertion; and Marta, who was new at the jail and joined the workshop the day of my first visit.

"Zechariah, chapter seven, verse nine." Visitación cleared her throat and read aloud: "Thus speaketh the Lord of hosts, saying, Execute true judgment, and shew mercy and compassions every man to his brother."

The women, weakened by hunger and exhaustion, barely said a word.

Visitación coughed and searched for another passage in her worse-for-wear, blackened Bible.

"Here it is! Saint Matthew! The healing of the blind near Jericho!" she read ceremoniously: "Have mercy on us, O Lord, thou son of David! And Jesus stood still, and called to them, and said, What will ye that I shall do unto you? They said unto him, Lord, that our eyes may be opened."

She paused dramatically before continuing. All the women were looking at her, lost in who knew what thought.

"What does this evangelist say to you?"

There was total silence, until one of the inmates raised her hand and made a halting summary of what Visitación had read out to them.

"No, Lorca! It's not *function*, it's *unction*!"

With those words ringing in my head, I wondered what purpose these visions of Messiahs who never came down to earth served. Visitación continued asking questions about the "word of God," her pompous way of referring to the Bible.

"Marta," she asked the new inmate, "What do you think about the blind from Jericho?"

No response.

"We're waiting."

"I don't like to speak."

As soon as she stopped shielding part of her face with her hand, I recognized her. My first impulse was to wrench out another tuft of her hair, but I controlled myself.

"Let's take a five-minute break to sort out this month's treats, which we will share with Marta," proposed Visitación.

She turned around and scolded me softly.

"What's wrong? Anyone would say you had seen a ghost." She regarded me with suspicion. "Take the new girl one of the bags. Don't ask or say anything. Let me be the one to talk."

I went over with a bundle of cigarettes and half a bread roll wrapped in a plastic bag. She was the last one to receive it. Her nails were dirty, she smelled of sweat, and she looked thinner, though she still had the same rodent eyes, sunken in her ghostly face.

Visitación resumed the workshop with a passage about regret.

"If Jesus, our Lord, was able to forgive, I ask that you have a good think about who you must forgive, and who must forgive you."

When the guards arrived to escort the inmates back to their cells, Marta, if that really was her name, shot a dark, saddened look my way.

I went over to her, under the pretense of giving her a print of the Virgin.

"You stole my documents and everything I had . . . ," I murmured. "May the God you believe in forgive you, because I certainly don't intend to."

The guards prodded the inmates as they herded them along, not giving them time to say goodbye. Marta looked at me in silence and, like the rest, left without saying a word. When we were in the pickup, right before the highway to Mezquite, Visitación made things very clear to me.

"This is the first and last time I'm bringing you here. We came here to bring these women some peace, not to frighten them. And you have sown mistrust. It would be best if we left it there."

I nodded, my head resting on the window. Visitación grabbed the car lighter and lit one of her small cigars.

"I'm going to Mezquite, shall I drop you at the cemetery or do you want to come with me?"

I was sure. It was her. I could never forget that face.

"Angustias, m'hija, Tolvaneras, or are you coming to town?"

I emerged from my daydream.

"Tolvaneras. I've got work to do."

I slipped my hands in my pockets. The jaguars were still there.

Visitación got a call from Puerta Grande jail. The guards had found the lifeless body of Marta Fernández Fernández. Her head was wrapped in a plastic bag. The autopsy ruled out foul play.

They searched for family members who could take the body but only found a mentally handicapped sister, interned in the Cucaña psychiatric hospital, who had recently been transferred to a hospital on the other side of the border. It had been six months since the fees to keep her at the center had been paid.

"That was why she was stealing . . . !"

"What's that, Angustias?"

"Nothing . . ."

"I'll be back in an hour. Have everything ready; we'll bury her this afternoon."

After churning the cement, I scoured the weeds for a stick of carnation, which had only meager yellow buds. They tolerated the lack of water and enlivened the blocks of concrete. I thought about her sister and how a death can condemn the life of another. I walked over to my sons' grave. I placed a toy horse next to the flowers.

Visitación arrived three hours later. After lowering the body out of the pickup, we placed it in a wooden casket I had nailed together the month before. She had a wooden box, at least; my sons only had cardboard boxes, the same ones she tried to steal at that shelter full of dying people and cockroaches.

With the same hand I had used to tear out a tuft of her hair in Cucaña, I wrote her name and date of birth on line number 750 of

The Third Country's burial register. I thought about the vengeful God Visitación praised so much, who cared not a whit about any of us down here. I wanted nothing from Him because He had never given me a thing.

"What are you thinking about, Angustias?"

"About this woman's sister."

"Nothing else?"

"No, Visitación, nothing else."

The first Sunday in May, two people held Cruz de Mayo celebrations: Abundio, at his hacienda for invitees only, and Visitación, for all the children in town. Visitación's was the most cheerful Cruz de Mayo celebration in the mountains.

Before nine, the Black woman crossed the market wearing her colorful headscarf and gathered a bunch of kids to cut the Palo de Mayo, which could be any length of wood, so long as it was thick. With that they constructed a tall cross, which they then adorned with glory flowers, hibiscus bouquets, and wild daisies that the children tied with ribbons and colorful paper.

The neighbors prepared aguapanela and served it in plastic cups or pewter mugs they brought from home. The bakers baked catalinas, cookies made from cinnamon and anise; naiboas too—cassava cakes covered in molasses that were consumed with white cheese. The market butchers carved up whole slabs of meat to roast on the fire, offering them as their contribution to the fiesta.

We ate at tables covered in colorful tablecloths. Green, blue, white, red. Lengths of fabric the women washed and hung out in the sun to dry afterward. Two people were needed then, one at each end. They stepped forward and backward, until they had folded them flaglike, in the form of a triangle. And that was how the tablecloths were kept until the following year, together with the petals and colorful ribbons that the children carefully retrieved from the Palo de Mayo. I was in charge of gathering all they collected and keeping a record of who had gathered the most flowers.

"You must be Angustias!"

I looked up from the notebook where I was jotting down names and the number of ribbons each had collected. A tall, corpulent woman stood before me, holding a small boy. She was dark skinned, and her hips were firm and shapely. Her yellow dress made her skin seem darker and glossier.

"Mamá won't stop talking about you! Jennifer, come here!" she called out to a solid woman with big arms.

"But . . . who is your mother?" I managed to ask.

"Who else? Visitación! We're the very picture of her! Can't you see it?"

They did look alike.

"I'm Mayerlin!" She curtsied in greeting, as if she were five years old. "Here comes my younger sister."

Both had thick hair. I hadn't seen heads of hair like that since I left the eastern mountains.

"I'm Jennifer." The other joined us. She too was well-built, like her mother. "Would you like some?"

She held out a cup of rum and aguapanela.

"No, thanks."

"Don't be a drag! Have a drink, it's delicious!"

She took a sip, then another, and went on like that until the glass was half-empty.

"Look at you, you're so young!"

"And pretty!" the other added.

They spoke breathlessly, constantly interrupting each other without ever giving me a chance to respond.

"Hurry up, m'hija, the dance is starting!"

"Ay, we love a good time! Come on!"

The two women laughed. I tried to get out of it, but they

dragged me to the square, where a group of men and women had formed a circle and were clinking glasses filled with rum and guarapo spiced with cinnamon.

"I'll introduce you to my husband."

"And I'll introduce you to mine."

"Me first! I'm the eldest!" bickered Mayerlin. "Don't worry about Mamá, by the way, she loves to be boss."

"We, on the other hand, love to party!" the larger one responded. "How nice to be back in town!"

The feast of the crosses, or Velorio de Mayo, as it was called in the mountains, brought back anyone who had moved away. It marked the beginning of the rainy season, the season that most resembled winter in the western mountains. Even if there was only a light drizzle, the water revived everything, including people's spirits. A life-giving moss that crept, little by little, over the stones.

The evening before the festivity, Mezquite smelled like sugar and melcocha, those sweet molasses straps that were left to rest beneath cloths, imbuing the kitchens with an old, treacly musk. Women from the eastern mountains who had arrived there before the plague prepared quark and majarete, a corn pudding; caramelized banana too. The smell covered everything with a steamy mist that escaped the pots sitting on the windowsills.

The banana jam, cooked over a low flame with water and aguapanela, was the highlight. It had to be fried properly and served with rice pudding, which children ate by the spoonful. "Oh rice pudding, I want to marry a widow from the city. May she know how to sew, how to embroider, and how to set the table forever after," they chanted, their bellies full, before clambering onto the rusty swings in the park.

Together with the flower-covered cross appeared Visitación, wearing a voluminous skirt, beneath which she had hidden two cushions to pantomime a donkey. She chased after the little ones, letting fly kicks and bucking about. The children tried to tear off her disguise. She never let them reach her, and held down her skirt as she ran, braying like an escapee from the corral.

"Visitación, it's you! We know it's you!" the children shouted.

When she tired of running to and fro, she took a seat and sang stanzas from "Saint John's Timber," a song everyone knew by heart, having repeated it for years. Jairo accompanied her on the accordion:

Sawdust, saw fast, Saint John's timber,
They ask for bread and don't get fed,
They ask for cheese and are given peas,
Ricki-ricki-ricki red.

Visitación's eldest daughter grabbed me by the waist, driving me toward a line of children and adults that advanced and retreated to the rhythm of "The Mezquite Snake." The song was always danced in a group, with everyone imitating the shape of a snake and responding, all together, to the calls Visitación sang loudly:

Here he comes.
Who?
He's getting close.
Who?
The mountain snake,
sambarambulé,

that wants to bite me,
sambarambulé.
If he bites me I'll kill him,
sambarambulé,
and make a scrawl out of him,
sambarambulé.
Holy Saint Anthony,
sambarambulé,
grant me strength,
sambarambulé,
to kill that snake,
sambarambulé,
that wants to bite me,
sambarambulé.

According to Palo de Mayo tradition, the person who collected the most ribbons and flowers would take home a pot of tamarind treacle and a cardboard diadem that I had covered in glitter. Everybody participated.

A girl prevailed over the rest. She alone managed to collect more ribbons and flowers than everybody else put together. She handed over a bag of fabric where she had hidden the ribbons and fresh-cut hibiscus so nobody could steal them. It was Consuelo.

Before she was given her prize, a drunk, uncouth man appeared. He treated her like a dog.

"Stop playing! Bring me some guarapo!"

"Quit scolding her, today's a feast day!" I shouted. "If you're so thirsty, go find it yourself."

Annoyed, he lurched off and was soon lost in the crowd. I went over to the girl and fitted the crown on her head.

"You're the queen of Mezquite."

She looked at me, disappointed.

"And what's the use of that?"

The wind stirred up a cloud of colorful paper. The smell of rain was in the air. The May rains were about to arrive.

Visitación wrenched the shovel I was using to churn the cement out of my hands, grabbed my arm, and hauled me over to the shed. She turned off the generator, grabbed the wooden bar she used as a lock, and fit it into the hooks either side of the door. It wasn't yet daybreak, and the early-morning darkness meant I could barely make out a thing.

"What's going on?"

"Shhhhhh."

She put her index finger to her lips, lifted a latch hidden beneath the trough, and pushed me in without saying a word.

"But . . ."

"Shhhhhh."

She picked up the rifle, adjusted her belt and sheathed her machete, and hid too, closing the air vent very slowly.

"It's the irregulars," she murmured. "Don't make a sound, don't move, don't think."

No longer a murmur, the engines roared in our ears. The irregulars piled out, slamming the doors. We didn't know how many there were, could only hear their laughter as they moved through the cemetery. The closer their voices came, the more my hands trembled.

"Open up, Visitación!"

The night retreated from the sky and a few tentative rays of morning light shone through. The men were still stationed at the door, ready to force their way in. They dealt blow after blow with their rifle butts, until the lock and wooden bar broke apart. Inside the space, air barely circulated, and a whiff of dust almost transformed our mousetrap into a coffin.

"Come out, wherever you are!"

Huddled in the drain, we could only see the feet of two men. One was hobbling on a plastic prosthetic. The other one was wearing military boots. I tried, but I couldn't make out anything else.

They went through everything. They threw the equipment and trays to the ground. My throat stung and the dust made me want to cough. Visitación was sweating profusely, her clothes already soaked through.

"We didn't find the woman, Commander!" Someone hurried inside. His voice sounded familiar. It was slow and soft, with an eastern accent.

"I don't want to hear it! I want her here, and I want her alive! If you don't bring her to me, I'll rip out your tongue!"

"We searched the graves, but found nothing. . . ."

That accent, that voice. It was so familiar.

"You've mobilized twenty men in vain, Mono." The one-legged man spat on the floor. "Wasting gasoline on this bullshit is not what we're about."

"Shut up, Gutiérrez, or I'll shove that peg leg down your throat. And you!" he ordered. "That's fresh concrete outside, so she can't be far. Keep looking, for fuck's sake!"

The other two stayed inside, strolling around at whim.

"Was that the recruit from the eastern mountains?"

"There's a few. All the new recruits are from there. Abundio sent them."

"Is he the one who doesn't say much, the one with the knife?"

"I'm not sure."

"Well find out! Don't you know your men?"

The trucks roared. The sound of the engines mingled with the voices of the insurgents. It was hot. I was suffocating. I couldn't bear to be like this much longer. I tried to move my head into another position, but I couldn't stem the choking feeling. Visitación cupped a hand over my mouth.

"What's it gonna be, doña? Are you coming out or not?" he shouted. "Stop being so rude! Mono has dropped by to say hello, and he's the goat that takes the most pisses on the border! If you haven't hidden in a wall, tell me where I can find you."

"Commander!"

The new recruit came in again.

"Did you find her?"

"No."

"Have you searched the water tank?"

"Not yet, Commander."

"Well hop to it! Open it up!"

Mono was vexed and shouted all his orders.

"No, no, no, no! Wait!" He changed his mind. "Shoot it up instead!"

"It's not worth it. Let it be," the one-legged man said in a conciliatory tone. "Our camp doesn't have enough munition to waste bullets on that. Leave the old lady and her dead alone."

"Will you keep looking, Gutiérrez?"

The boots came ever closer to the grate, until I could make out the mud caked on them. Mono was getting angrier, and he kicked the cabinet until it toppled. The shovels, mattocks, buckets, and ropes clattered across the floor.

"I want the old lady's hide, you understand?" He finished with a kick to the door. "I'm the one who decides what we do and don't do!"

"Whatever you say, Commander."

"I don't say, Gutiérrez. I order."

There was a stony, uncomfortable silence. Any noise, even a tiny one, would give us away.

"And in that case, doña? There's still time to come out. Don't make me do it my way."

Visitación closed her eyes and kept her hand over my mouth.

"You're here, I know it, the pickup outside is yours."

He grabbed a stick and hit the tin roof. *Tock! Tock! Tock!* If he kept it up, the roof would fall in.

"Are you up there? No, you couldn't be. Or do you hide in one of your graves?"

My throat was prickling, and as much as I tried to contain it, a cough would escape at any moment. Visitación pressed her hand against my mouth even tighter. We heard another sound, soft at first, and then louder: liquid spraying the floor. It slid across the cement and then started trickling into the vent. It was urine.

"Next time, Visitación, I'll be pissing gasoline!" the man shouted. "Then I'll light a cigar and use your face as my ashtray!"

Covered in piss, terrified out of our minds, we waited in silence for the men to lift the latch and kill us.

"Commander!"

The new recruit came in for the third time, at a clip, carrying several tools.

"Commander!" he insisted. "We shot up the tank! We left it like a colander!" He could barely speak.

"And what? Was she inside?"

"No, but lots of shit came out," he panted. "A whole heap of huge snakes . . . like the ones down at the swamp."

"You pussy. . . . The swamp dried up years ago!"

"They're all over the place. We've killed some with our machetes, but more and more are coming out. The men don't want to open the graves! They all think this is the devil's work!"

"You fucking whore, Visitación! You witch! When I get my hands on you, I'll kill you! I swear it!"

"You have to come see this."

A swift, metallic sound pierced our ears. It sounded like a pistol safety catch.

"Get out of here!"

"Don't shoot, please," begged the private.

"Outside, or I'll blow your head off!"

First the one-legged man left, then the soldier. Mono stayed a few minutes more. Before leaving the shed, he fired three bullets at the metal door.

"Next time I'll be using you for target practice, Visitación. Leave this place on your own two feet. Don't make me come find you. If I have to, I'll fuck you over."

We could hear his steps headed for the door.

Mono and his men left swiftly. Only after the slams of car doors and the rumble of engines traveling toward the highway did Visitación remove her hand from my mouth. I coughed for several minutes. I had an unbearable itch in my throat and nose.

We crept out of our hiding place with the coming of the light. Once outside, I ran to the tap, put my lips to it, and drank without pause. I filled a mug and took it to Visitación, who had sat down beneath the spiny holdback.

"Fear makes us thirsty, doesn't it, m'hija?" She tied on her colorful headscarf as she shooed away the wasps circling her.

Maimed by machetes, snakes were writhing everywhere. Disembodied heads were biting tails, which lashed the sand like whips. I could smell filth and charcoal. Glinting in the first light of day, a small knife lay in the sand. It was crude, resembling a burin.

Visitación started laughing.

"When I first came here, I sealed the well because it drew dirty water from the swamps. And look what was inside!"

I quickly slipped the knife into my pocket and nodded.

"The souls from the next world must truly care for me!" she shouted.

I didn't know if it was the wind or my fear making me hear things, but I thought I heard laughter coming from the middle of nowhere.

The irregulars hadn't had time to open the graves. They were all intact. When we finished examining the grave-yard, Visitación stood before the only grave in the cemetery without a date. It only had a first name, no last: Gloria. Its headstone was small, painted indigo, and it had a plastic rose embedded in the cement.

"She was the first one to come to The Third Country." Visitación wiped her forehead with the back of her hand. "Before all this, I had my dead buried in a small section of the Central Cemetery. But in Mezquite, the winter intensified, and downpours washed the soil away, exposing them. I had to take them out of there."

A gust of wind sullied our chapped skin with sand.

"I got written permission, placed them in bags, and brought them to this place."

Visitación had a habit of choosing the most roundabout way of explaining the simplest of things. I had no idea what she was on about.

"They're all up in arms. They hate me having my dead here. . . . Tolvaneras belongs to nobody. It belongs to Gloria, to your sons, to all those who are at rest here. . . ." She raised her hands and motioned at the graves. "They are the owners of all this! Not Abundio, not the priest! Not even I! They are! This land belongs to the dead!"

"The irregulars almost killed us this morning, Visitación."

"It's not the first time they've come here. And it won't be the last."

"They mentioned Abundio. That man has eyes everywhere. What does he want?"

"Everything, my dear. He wants everything."

"If he hates you so much, why doesn't *he* come and drag you away?"

"These irregulars weren't sent by Abundio! They came alone, to take me away from here feetfirst, and have all this to themselves, without sharing it with anybody, you understand?"

I looked at my calloused hands, which were almost as chapped as hers.

"I don't like what's happening here," I said. "You've got issues with everyone: the mayor, the irregulars, the man with the dogs. And you don't explain anything to me."

Visitación turned around and pointed a finger at me.

"I warned you. The gate's right there. But if you leave, then that's that, there's no coming back."

She sipped a little more water and looked at me, mistrustful.

"With me or against me. That's how things are on this side of the mountains. Think it over!"

She left, dragging her feet, headed for the shed. She examined the bullet holes in the metal door and went inside to clean up all trace of the men.

We didn't say another word to each other for the rest of the day.

After gathering up and burning the dead snakes, I headed over to my sons' grave. I found another two figures carved in wood, one for each son. They were fish, small and simple, like the jaguars. I hadn't put them there. Except for the irregulars, nobody had visited the cemetery that week.

The figurines still in hand, I pulled out the knife I had found on the ground, but it was too crude, and the blade was thicker than the furrows in the little figures. The accent from the eastern mountains echoed in my ears. The voice was Salveiro's, who else could it be?

I shook my head to dispel the echo of a man who should have been dead. I inspected the graves one by one but found nothing out of place. Sliding the knife back in my pocket, together with my scissors, I returned the fish to where I had found them. Hiding them wouldn't change a thing.

I sat down before the grave again, not knowing what to do.

The wind ruffled my hair. It had grown.

Visitación Salazar had her eyes fixed on a pot of water near boiling.

"But look who's here!" she shouted, raising her arms. "I thought you'd left."

"And I thought you were in Mezquite, with your boyfriend."

"Come off it!" She paused. "Víctor Hugo can be a bit hopeless. He needs to stand on his own two feet for once. I can't always be at his beck and call." She ladled water into a cloth filter heaped with ground coffee. "Plus, girl, I'm staying because I feel like it. . . . I don't owe an explanation to anybody. Not to him, not to you."

I sat next to her.

"Coffee?"

I nodded.

"I shouldn't," murmured Visitación. "The last few nights I haven't slept. . . ."

"What's keeping you awake?"

"All this." She sighed, defeated.

A truck sped down the highway, headed north. Visitación got up, grabbed the flashlight, and walked to the gate. She locked it and turned off the gate lamp. She came back, light shining on the wire fence, and plopped onto the stool by the electric cooker.

"Today you accused me of telling you nothing. . . ."

"It's the truth, Visitación. And this doesn't feel right to me."

"Girl, I can't believe you've buried two boys and still act like you were born yesterday."

"Come now, I treat you with respect."

Visitación lowered her gaze, removed the cloth filter, and ladled more water.

"It's a long story. . . ." She served the coffee, offering a cup to me. "Sure you want to hear it?"

I nodded.

"Estigia Ágave traveled to Mezquite to marry Francisco Fabres. She was an educated woman, the eldest daughter of a manufacturing family that had money. Francisco was heir to the old textile mills and the most important yarn factory in the mountains."

She added more water to the filter and stirred the coffee.

"Amalia, my mother, worked for that family for a long time. She was in charge of the cooking and anything else that needed doing: She tended the kitchen garden and planned meals for everyone. She fed two generations in that house."

The glow of the burner attracted bugs: midges, moths, and black ants that had delicate wings and got caught in our clothes. Visitación kept batting away the insects with her hand. She poured herself a mug of black coffee and continued.

"My mother respected Doña Estigia. She said she was intelligent and well organized, very enterprising. She had a census done to find out how many working-age citizens lived in Mezquite and how many could be employed in the new textile mills. The year she was married, after she had started the factory, Estigia gave birth to three girls with fair skin and black hair."

I didn't understand why she was telling me this old story, nor what I was meant to take away from it. We were almost killed, and she came out with this? But, as always, she paid me no mind.

"When Estigia went to the textile mills to put everything in order, my mother stayed with the little girls. Everything in that house revolved around the business: even the girls developed a taste for fabric and fibers," she said, solemn. "The Fabreses knew all there was to know about cotton. What happened in their work-shops influenced town life! In Mezquite, everybody found work with them; it was decent work too: as operators, unloaders, drivers . . . and it was well paid."

I heard a sound near the gate.

"Leave it, Angustias, it's just the goats." Visitación carried on with her story: "The Fabreses supplied the whole border region with fabric. They were already rich, but they grew even richer. The daughters inherited the fortune and power of the family. But they didn't know how to defend it."

I heard more noises. I was afraid a snake might be lurking in the bushes.

"When the triplets became young ladies, Estigia sent them to study in the capital."

Visitación took a cigarette from her pocket, one of the ones they sold loose in the market. She lit it on the burner and took a deep drag.

"Everything was going well but . . . ayyyyy!"

She howled dramatically, like a mourner at a wake. I thought something had bitten her.

"What is it? What's wrong?"

"The Cumboto broke its banks!"

My heart was still beating in my throat. She'd given me such a fright!

"The river took a piece of the mountain with it, and then dumped it on the textile mill premises. Everything was trans-formed into a quagmire." She looked at my mug. "You don't drink coffee? Or isn't it any good?"

I forced down a sip.

"Keep going."

"That was a tragedy . . . and then Abundio, who could sniff out weakness the way piranhas smell blood, showed up on the Fabreses' doorstep." She stood up, her arms akimbo, to imitate him. "'If it doesn't produce it's done away with!' he shouted, brandishing his pistol. Don Francisco came out to meet him. Estigia refused to give him the honor, so she stayed in her bedroom. The men were in the office for half an hour. . . ." She pointed to a nonexistent watch on her wrist. "They came out in silence. Estigia Ágave stood in their way. Acting gallant, Abundio stretched out his hand, but she wouldn't take it. . . . I'm telling you this just the way my mother told me, she was the one who saw Abundio to the door. That was why he hated her—she saw everything that happened."

Fabres had offered Abundio the textile mill sites, in exchange for not touching the house, the only thing the bank had not taken. Abundio thought the properties weren't sufficient and, after placing his pistol on the desk, asked to marry one of the sisters, so he could have her share too.

The wedding celebration of Mercedes Fabres Ágave and Alcides Abundio was an intimate affair. The priest, the provincial governor, a notary, and a few distant relatives were present. None of the district traders attended; they regarded the expropriation and union with horror. Her sisters did not attend either. The most acute absence was that of Estigia Ágave, who two weeks before had thrown herself into the Cumboto, each ankle weighed down by stones.

"The marriage produced a girl, Carmen. She was the only child of that unfortunate union." Visitación put out her cigarette and covered it in sand. "Who knows if he violated his wife to end up with everything, including this land here. But I reclaimed it as my own because Abundio owed it to my mother. He threw her out without paying her a cent, after she had worked there for thirty years!"

She raised her mug, finished the last sip of coffee, and threw the grounds onto the sand.

"I'm going to bed. Switch everything off, we don't want to be spotted, at least not tonight."

She left, troubled, her hands on her hips. I lingered a while longer. That story seemed remote, a flight of fancy. I touched the knife I still had in my pocket and drank a little more of the black coffee to put my questions to rest, but they were still there, like nails buried in my head.

Sitting before the burner, I heard a pygmy owl with its woeful cry. Something bad was about to happen. If it had not happened already, that was.

After marrying Mercedes, Abundio was not only the chief administrator of the textile mills and farms: he also established himself as the new owner. He dismissed many of the workers and trusted staff, and instead of repairing the broken machinery, sold it for scrap before converting the old factory buildings into storage facilities. He looted the factory and destroyed everything. Later, he would off-load all his resentment onto his daughter. He was boiling with rage for not having fathered a boy, but at least the little girl ensured him a portion of the lands belonging to his wife, whom he subjected to ferocious surveillance.

Before anointing him mayor of Mezquite, Abundio entrusted Aurelio Ortiz with a few tasks to determine whether he was loyal or cowardly. Spying on Mercedes was the first assignment. Aurelio had just married Salvación. He needed the money, so he accepted without a second thought.

He materialized before his boss's wife one night, in the middle of the first downpour that winter. Mercedes had returned from one of her trips to her childhood home, where she was spending more and more time with her daughter, Carmen, who was three or four at that point.

"Aurelio Ortiz, at your service."

She looked him up and down.

"People don't serve me, they work for me. Anything else is more my husband's style. I see; he's the one who sent you."

Aurelio nodded.

"Instead of wasting your time, tell Alcides I don't need chaperones or spies."

It was the same thing his own wife had told him.

"So now you're a snitch? I don't know why you go along with this kind of thing, Aurelio," Salvación had admonished him. "You would be better off opening an accounting firm! Signing documents, recording sales! Something normal people do!"

His wife was stubborn and mistrustful. She never stopped berating him. Yet her heart was in the right place; she did not turn her nose up at any work, and she could be supportive. She was from San Fernando de las Salinas, a town on the coast about five or six hours from the mountains. She was tall, her body thick like a rain tree. She came to the mountains to open a new branch of her dietary franchise. Through it, she dispensed miracle powders with pitches as extravagant as their names: JowlBeGone, BellyBuster, NewLeaseOnLife. Even Visitación bought some of her herbal concoctions.

Nobody could deceive her because she was skeptical about everything. She needed very little information to understand how things were. That was why she did not like to see her husband work for Abundio. She was right, but he was not about to grant her that.

Mercedes knew the talk: Abundio visited whores, bred fighting cocks, drank aguardiente with his workers, and committed atrocities on the land that was once her family's. None of it mattered. Nor did the watchful scrutiny she was submitted to, day and night. Her only concern had a name: Críspulo Miranda. She did not like the way he looked at Carmen, or the way he moved freely about the house.

"It's Críspulo or us, you choose!"

Abundio got up out of the chair and walked around the desk, his boots sounding. He came to a stop before his wife and slapped her so hard she saw stars.

"Go wherever you want, but Carmen stays here. She's mine!"

Mercedes smoothed her clothes and stood her ground.

"We'll see about that." And she spat on him.

Crouched between two stone water filters, Aurelio saw her come out of the office, a dark, bitter expression on her face. The rain pelted the shingles and the wind knocked over some flowerpots. She continued without registering his presence. Nor did she notice Críspulo, who was sharpening a machete with a whetstone.

A flash of lightning tore the man from the darkness. Mercedes stopped short. He dropped the machete to the ground and pointed at her. When she leaned in, trying to decipher what he was trying to tell her, a red drop fell from her nose and spotted her white blouse, like a period.

t was still early, and only a few people were wandering the market aisles. I bought colorful pinwheels for Higinio and Salustio's grave, and went to the tire fitter's, on an errand from Visitación.

"The two tires are ready. Tell Visitación one of them is on me. She knows why."

He handed me back half the money.

I heaved the new tires onto the bed. I was thirsty and I was tired, yet I preferred to get back to Tolvaneras as soon as possible. There was still work to be done. Just before I opened the pickup door, I heard shouting.

"Come! Come here! I don't have all day!"

It was the man I had seen with Consuelo before. He was shouting up and down the street, drunk like last time. Consuelo was trying to push some boxes crammed with junk.

"Pick them up, stupid!" he kept shouting. "And don't drop anything!"

Walking beside them were men and women shouldering backpacks. Everybody was hauling mats and tents. They must have been going from town to town, picking over trash and reselling whatever they found.

"Don't drag the stuff, I told you!"

I didn't like his ways. Somebody had to show him Consuelo wasn't alone.

"Hey! Lower your voice. No need to shout."

"And who the hell are you?"

"Watch your tone. And treat the girl with a little respect."

"Keep out of it!"

"Don't raise your voice at me. And if you keep up this racket, I'll call the police. We'll see if they don't deport you for disorderly conduct and pickpocketing."

The man turned tail and hurried to gather up his junk. I moved closer to Consuelo as quickly as possible and reached into my pocket for the bills the tire fitter had given me.

"Hide them! If you come back to Mezquite, come find me. I'm here every Tuesday and Thursday."

Consuelo tucked the money away swiftly. She had more shaving nicks on her head, and she was nothing but skin and bone.

"I've got to go, I'm needed!"

She headed down the street, carrying comforters that smelled like goats. She had lost the haughty air of a girl from the coast and was now a shadow of her former self. The border was devouring her bite by bite. Quite possibly it was doing the same to me.

We turned off the interstate to find something to eat. We entered Mezquite along the main street, which at that time of day was full of hawkers and food stalls where people were eating arepas stuffed with crackling and meat, taro, and vegetable soup for lunch.

"My stomach's grumbling!" Visitación flicked on the turn signal and pulled into a no-standing zone. "Hurry up, Angustias! I can't drive to Nopales on an empty stomach!"

We crossed the road against the light.

"Visitación! Take me to heaven, mamita!" two teenagers cried.

She let out a laugh, proud and haughty. She was impossible to miss: her joyous laughter, her tight clothing, her headscarf, and those firm legs. More than inhabit the world, Visitación magnetized it. And she knew it.

"I'll lend you my wings to take you there!" she responded, flirty, and slowed her pace.

"Weren't you dying of hunger just a second ago?"

"No need to be jealous, Angustias, let them get a good look. . . ."

Usually, the popular chicken rotisserie was packed at all hours, but that day there were barely any patrons. At the back, the chickens were turning on a spike, inside a gas spit roaster.

"Chúo, my love, give me two of those and a yucca! And make it quick, papito!"

"Do you have a job to get to, doña?"

"A dearly departed in Nopales." She leaned on the bar. "Make sure you cut those chickens properly, Chúo, don't leave too much bone! And give me two chilled beers, but make those for right now, honey."

"Whatever you say, gorgeous."

He was missing an eye. Another game-fowl breeder.

Visitación grabbed the cans, popped the tab on her own, and took a long swig. She wiped her mouth with the crumpled handkerchief she had tucked into her waistband.

"Drink, m'hija, you're as withered as a stick. Look at me, this body of mine is pure energy!"

She lit a smoke and leaned back on the bar, the cigarette in one hand and her beer in the other.

"What do you think of this insanity?"

"What do you mean?"

"This, making a living burying the dead."

She took another sip.

"You have learned to work and smooth the concrete, but you still don't know the most important thing about burying the dead."

"And what's that?"

"Being alive! But you're oblivious. You don't sleep, don't eat, don't drink."

"I leave that to you. You do it best."

"Now, now, Angustias, I see what you're up to!" She turned around. "Chúo, one small chicken to have here, I'll share it with Angustias!"

She grew serious; it was clear she was about to get on her soapbox.

"I eat when I'm hungry and laugh because I like to. It's inside me. That's why my boyfriend fell in love with me: I enjoy life, I know all about life and death."

She smiled and patted her hips.

At sixty years of age, she was right to flaunt it. After separating from her husband, she had two or three boyfriends, all of them young. She had twenty years on Víctor Hugo. The man was meek and gossipy, but she didn't care about that. They did not even live together—she didn't want to.

"I've already raised a son! So I said to Víctor Hugo: 'Look, babe, I like men who take care of their appearance, who take care of themselves. If you want, we can make this official. . . .'"

By the third drink, her tongue loosened.

"Víctor Hugo is a bit slow on the uptake, and everything has to be explained to him in simple terms, but he's capable in bed. Aside from his gambling, he does as he's told . . . and that's important. A good fuck makes you feel alive, Angustias. And you're not getting any. You're like a nun. *Sister* Angustias! Sister Angustias!"

Here she goes again, I thought.

"I've buried countless bodies, and it's made me realize we got to use the one we're given." She looked to one side and then the other as she blew two plumes of smoke out her nose. "I know a lot, and I share my knowledge. . . . You know what I mean!" She patted her crotch.

I drank my beer because at this rate she would soon toss back mine too, and we still had a way to travel.

"That's it, Angustias, bottoms up!" She bumped her can against mine. "Cheers! I don't do this every day, only every now and then. . . ." She put on a pious face and continued with her sermon: "When people come to a cemetery, they feel afraid. It's ugly, it's strange. But those who come to The Third Country want to stay because peace reigns there. . . . For me, the living and the dead are one and the same. Not everyone gets the chance to be born, but everyone will die one day."

A steaming-hot chicken on a paper plate was set before us. Visitación leaned over it.

"Ayyyyy, Chuito, this is finger-licking good!" When she chewed, her mouth looked bigger. "Would you like some, Sister Angustias? Or are you fasting?" I shook my head. "You can't live on air alone. You talk, live, and think like you're a hundred years old."

The sound of her teeth as she ground the cartilage reverberated in my ears. Grease was covering her mouth, as if she had applied lipstick made of lard.

"And you . . . you don't miss it?"

"Chicken?"

"Don't play innocent—you know what I'm talking about. Your husband wasn't bad, and he was a big man."

"What one man gives, any can. You said so yourself."

"You don't need to take what I say so literally."

"Look who's talking, the Virgin of Tolvaneras!"

Visitación let out one of her laughs.

"Chúo, the check!" She took another bite of the chicken breast and finished her beer. "Let's go, otherwise I'll get a fine for parking in a no-standing zone!"

On our way to the door, Críspulo Miranda intercepted us.

"Good afternoon, ladies."

"Where are your dogs? You don't have them with you today?"

"Hunger does them good. You would know all about that, wouldn't you?" he was addressing me.

"You're a bastard, Críspulo. Out of the way, Indian, I don't feel like beating up anyone today."

The man stepped aside, scrutinizing us with his snake eyes.

"You'd best be careful. The road to Nopales is crawling with thugs, and two women on their own . . ."

NO PLACE TO BURY THE DEAD

At the sound of his voice, I spun around.

"And what do you care where we're headed!"

"Críspulo is all seeing, Angustias."

We stepped out into the street smelling like grease and smoke. Like prey.

Angustias! Quit shouting!"

My cheek still stinging, I rubbed my eyes.

"Ow, don't be so brutal!"

"You'd sleep better if you had a good fuck. You need an outlet, woman!" Visitación berated me.

Since the wooden jaguars first appeared on the boys' grave I could barely sleep, and when I did, I had strange dreams: Virgins that gave birth to tigers, Mary Immaculates that cradled ocelot cubs in their arms, Paso Fino horses that exploded, disintegrating in the air like bits of shredded beef. But this dream was different. I was walking around The Third Country, my hairdressing scissors in hand. I was barefoot, and a skirt made of iridescent snakes hung from my waist. The wind made them ripple, like a fine silk spun from scales and venom.

In the distance I could hear barks, but I felt invincible beneath my armor of hungry vipers. When I arrived at my sons' grave, I came across a man praying on his knees.

"Get out of here!" I shouted without needing to open my mouth, like a wrathful Virgin.

He didn't even turn.

"Speak! What do you want?"

Rage rippled through my body. The snakes peeled off my waist like unraveling threads and set upon him until he was immobilized. On my feet, and naked from the waist down, I watched them break his bones. One by one.

Sweet Jesus! Why right now? Damn traffic!" Visitación pitched a butt out the window.

Trucks and cars idled at a standstill, clogging the interstate, which was crawling with buses, dry-goods trucks, and military convoys. Visitación lit another cigarette, inhaled, and exhaled smoke like a dragon.

"Be prepared, Angustias. We're about to arrive in the ugliest town in the mountains."

"Which of them isn't?"

Nopales was full of dive bars and cockpits, and while both these enterprises pervaded the border region, here they were distinct because they benefited from Abundio's protection. He sent his best specimens to Nopales's cockpits: ferocious, eye-catching fowls, creatures with red eyes, erect crests, and strong beaks.

Nobody could resist the cheap spectacle of watching something die, especially at those fights drowned in blood and anisette, the town's main source of revenue. Abundio had converted Nopales into a laboratory. He introduced variations to the bouts and took a cut of all the bets. Even when he lost, he won.

Of all the bouts, he most enjoyed a version that he had invented, which had caused an immediate outcry across the mountains. Called The Beach, it was simple but effective. He gathered around twenty of his weakest farmhands to lie on the sand, prostrate and naked. Anybody who came to the arena would get a laugh out of recognizing one or two. Members of the crowd filmed them and cracked lewd jokes.

Once the bell sounded, the hollering began. The game fowls

dealt pecks as they traversed a carpet of naked and frightened men who barely understood what was happening. They covered their heads in desperation, forced into a kind of purgatory. Most were anesthetized by alcohol. Others died during the fight, exhausted and defeated, knocking on hell's door.

The bets, the animal trafficking, and the settling of accounts between criminal factions condemned the inhabitants of Nopales to live locked up in their houses, just as afraid of the locals as they were of the out-of-towners. Except for the cockpits, Nopales had almost nothing. There were no clinics, no schools. Children were sent to Mezquite and Villalpando, although almost all of them left their studies and ended up sicarios. They never learned to read, but when it came to death, they knew all there was to know.

The town had a square, a church, a dilapidated town hall, a bar-lined street, and a market where people sold reptiles, macaws, venomous frogs, game fowl, monkeys, and electric eels that killed horses when they drank from Cumboto watering holes.

La Niña Muerta was its patron saint, a cadaverous Virgin who protected the traders of that lawless bazaar: a skeleton dressed as a bride, crowned with a halo of white flame. People referred to her as the Virgin of the Forsaken. The sicarios placed their fates in her hands and made prayers in her name. The offertory included animals, bottles of aguardiente, milk teeth, and sugar-glazed white sweets that were known as saints' bones. Her devotees considered as a given some of her divine gifts—like finding things that had gone missing—in exchange for a penance that brooked no lapses. Otherwise, she came back to reclaim the dark miracle of her favor.

A foul, dry wind guided us to town. After a few minutes' stroll, we reached Candelaria Macario's house. The door had a Sacred Heart adorned by a garland of snake plant, a plant attributed medicinal properties by the people in the mountains and displayed in their homes to ward off sickness.

Candelaria was seventy. She was blind and gaunt. She had devoted her life to Jesús, her only child. When the doctors diagnosed him with leukemia, she nursed him as if he were a part of her, an appendage that would inevitably be amputated one day.

That was why we were there. To wrap them in a shroud. Her and him.

We made our way down a hallway lined with ferns and shelves. Guided by the light at the end of the passage, we reached a living room furnished with three chairs and a side table, atop which lay clay trinkets and faded photos.

"Candelaria, I'm Visitación!"

"Keep coming, it's this way!" cried the woman from the end of another hall.

We stopped before a dark bedroom. After we switched on the light, a weak, flickering bulb dimly lit the space. The elderly woman held a young man in her arms. She looked like a blind Virgin dressed in a housecoat. Candelaria kept her hands on her son's face. With her fingertips, she committed the contours of his dead flesh to memory.

"He left this world at three in the afternoon. There you have the papers." Visitación searched for the folder and looked at the medical examiner's documents. "You will be the one to bury him, is that right?"

"That's what I'm here for." The naked bulb fizzed. "Candelaria, go get some rest."

"I don't want to," she answered, not lifting her hands from her son's face.

"I'll stay with him until daybreak," said Visitación.

"I'm not budging an inch."

I stepped forward.

"Candelaria, get some rest, and let him do the same."

The woman raised her head, sniffing the air.

"Are you Angustias Romero?"

"Yes."

The room smelled of medicine and sweat.

"They say you've moved to Tolvaneras to live there with your dead sons. Is that right?"

"It is."

"Then don't ask me to do with mine what you haven't done with yours."

The roosters crowed, disoriented. They were not calling forth the day, only frightening off death.

When she finally gave in, Candelaria slept like a log. I escorted her to the bed and placed her false teeth in a glass of water and bicarbonate soda. Without them, she looked like a baby ready for the grave.

Visitación prepared Jesús's body. His clothing was steeped in the sour odor that dying people exude before they leave this world. Between the two of us, we moved him to the dining room. Visitación held him beneath his arms, and I held him by the ankles. We lay him on the table.

"Take off his nightshirt, Angustias."

Stripped of that item of clothing, his body was now clad in only a diaper.

"He must have died some time before what his mother told us." Visitación bent his wrists. "He's a bit stiff."

She did the same with his elbow and fingers. His body emitted faint sounds, like crackles, signs that he was no longer of this earth.

"Careful," she cautioned. "Dampen the swabs properly. We don't have a drain here, so nothing can be spilled."

I removed a bottle of disinfectant from the metal box where we housed the instruments and soaked a cotton ball. Visitación used it to wipe the facial orifices, as well as the navel, underarms, and crotch.

"The nose is cleaned like this," she said, rubbing it, "and it is vacuumed after. Mouth hygiene is more delicate." His lips were violet and partially open. "Now he's going to tell us what he's like." Visitación covered her index finger with blotting paper and massaged his temples. "This is to revive his expression." Then she scraped a yellow layer from his tongue. "We have to avoid bacteria and odors." She shaved him, holding his jaw inside his mouth to stretch the skin. "If I cut him with the blade he won't bleed, but soon enough marks will appear."

She tore off another piece of blotting paper and removed the excess foam from his face. She searched for the comb in the box and carefully felt his hair. She went into the kitchen and came back with a damp cloth.

"When you wet it, the hair always tells a story."

She sank the comb into his hair and patiently started cutting it.

"Wait!" I pulled out my scissors.

I trimmed and evened out the hair on the nape of his neck, until it was bare. Visitación nodded and tamed the hair with a brush.

"The only difference between him and us is the act of breathing. You and I can still do it. He no longer can."

Her movements were confident and precise. She took her time arranging his hands and brought his feet together.

"In just a few hours, Angustias, we have to give back to the dead some of what life has taken away. The main thing is that they look like they belong to this world, even though they no longer do. Understand?" I nodded. "We have to work miracles. When his mother wakes, she needs to find him almost alive."

"But Candelaria is blind."

"Nobody would believe you know what it's like to bury a son. He needs to smell like soap! When she touches his hair, it needs to be damp! Like he has just stepped out of the shower!"

I nodded.

"Look for some fabric or paper, anything you can find, we need to make a cushion."

I pulled down the wreath of snake plant from the door. Visitación propped it beneath Jesús's head, like a pillow.

"We're done."

Candelaria was listening at the doorway. She looked like an owl. She came over to the table and lay her hands on her son's face. Her toothless mouth stretched into a smile.

"May God bless you, Visitación."

"Amen."

Visitación slammed on the brakes. Two pickups blocked access to The Third Country. Víctor Hugo was waiting with Reyes and Críspulo, who had his dogs with him once more.

"Víctor Hugo, m'hijo! What are you doing here? Open the gate!" she shouted, leaning half her torso out of the window. "Son of a bitch!"

She worked the clutch and rammed the barricade. She had lost her senses. Reyes let off a warning shot in the air. She reversed and rammed them again. The driver took another shot. The bullet struck the rearview mirror.

"Angustias, take the wheel and stay here with Candelaria! Don't get out till I say so!"

She jumped out of the cabin without anything to defend herself with, not even a shovel or a machete.

"The cemetery is closed." Reyes pointed his machine gun at her.

"We'll see about that! Open up, right now!"

"Until the mayor's decree is lifted, you can't bury any more people here. Calm down and take the old lady home," Reyes tried to reason with her.

"Aurelio Ortiz can come down here to tell me that. What's he doing? Off getting a manicure?"

"Have some respect, doña," the driver stopped her. "Today is payday, and Sir Aurelio is busy with contractors and employees."

"*Sir?*" She laughed angrily.

I searched for the shotgun beneath the seat. There weren't many shells, and I was not a good shot, but by that stage I didn't care.

"Candelaria, hunker down! I'll be right back."

I yanked the door handle and jumped out of the pickup. Visitación was still spoiling for a fight.

"Your boss—sorry, I mean *Sir Aurelio*—is busy? What a surprise!" She adjusted her headscarf. "So he's too scared to come in person to tell me he's closing The Third Country. It's a good thing your mother's dead, Críspulo! How embarrassing, giving birth to somebody like you!"

Críspulo stroked the German shepherd.

"No God will ever forgive you! Or Aurelio, or that traitor there!"

Víctor Hugo looked down when she pointed at him.

"What's wrong, papi? I don't lend you money for your gambling habit, but they do? When these people fill your mouth with flies, tell Beelzebub that the only good thing in your life was this."

Visitación clapped her hand between her legs and spun around to face Críspulo.

"If you're so brave, leave the dogs and come here! Fight with your own two hands!"

"Your boy opened the gate for us," Críspulo motioned toward Víctor Hugo, who was trembling like a leaf. "The man knows what's best for him, doñita. He's been telling us everything for a while now: what time you leave, when you come back, who comes to see you."

When I saw her make for him, her hand clenched, I took the safety off the shotgun. Críspulo released the lead of the German shepherd, and I pulled the trigger. The dog dropped dead, its head shattered like a walnut. I ran over to Visitación. She was covered in blood, I didn't know whether hers or the dog's.

"Are you hurt?"

"Not at all! Let go of me, I'm going to strangle Víctor Hugo! Traitor! Dirty slob! Toad! You'll pay for this, dammit!"

I shoved her into the cabin and reversed out. After two swerves, I joined the main road. In the rearview mirror, the three men still stood over the body of the German shepherd.

"Drive straight to Mezquite," she ordered. "There's nobody alive who can mess with Visitación Salazar! A mule kick doesn't kill the horse!"

"Visitación . . ."

"Shut up, Angustias, and do as I say."

She was completely out of her mind.

t was payday in Mezquite. People and money were moving quickly. The hawkers were clamoring in the main square and traders from across the mountains were dispatching their goods. We parked outside city hall. It was blocked by a line of men and women asking Aurelio Ortiz for a job, food, medicine. Anything.

"I'll be right back, Angustias."

"You're not going in alone!"

"Stay with Candelaria!"

"What are you going to do?"

"Justice, which is no small thing."

"Leave it. You're not moving from here." I grabbed her arm, but she broke free and started toward city hall again.

Jairo, who had come back to the market to sing, was standing before us, sustaining a single note on his accordion. Visitación pushed him aside.

"What's wrong? Where are you going, so fired up?"

"To go sing some truths to the mayor!"

"I'll provide the accompaniment if you like. . . ."

"Let me through, Jairo." Visitación smacked him one. "Don't make me fume."

"Okay." He raised his hands. "But listen to Angustias: let her go with you."

"I don't need her, you, or anyone!"

He walked over to Visitación's pickup and peered in the window.

"Candelaria!"

"May God bless you."

Visitación regarded him suspiciously.

"Are you done?"

"You go with Angustias, I'll stay with Candelaria."

"Doña, do you know this man?" asked Visitación.

The elderly woman nodded.

"Candelaria has just lost her son." She turned to Jairo. "So you be very careful if you go making up some tune. Wait here."

"You can count on that."

"You." Visitación turned to me. "Come with me."

She removed the tarp we had spread over the bed. The lifeless body of Jesús was visible, wrapped in its shroud, together with the ropes and shovels.

"You hold him by the arms, I'll take the feet!"

I didn't dare object.

The men and women waiting outside city hall surrounded us.

"What are you doing, Visitación? You're crazy!"

"Don't say that," somebody intervened. "Visitación always takes care of everybody else."

"Mind your own business!"

"You're putting everyone at risk with that body!"

"The woman with her brought the plague here!"

"And her husband goes around with the irregulars!"

"The two of them came from the eastern mountains! Go back to where you came from!"

A voice cut through the crowd.

"Shut up, everyone!"

It was Consuelo, or what was left of her. A belly of at least six months protruded from her bony, hungry body.

"We all know these women!" She pointed to Visitación and me. "They've given every single one of us something! You," she scolded a woman, "they brought you food! You," she barked at someone else, "they helped bury your wife, and asked for nothing in return! And now you're turning against them?"

"Why don't you go back over the mountains, you ungrateful bitch? Did Visitación get you your job at the dive bar too?"

"None of your business how I earn a living," snapped Consuelo.

"You smelly cow! Go calve in your own land!"

The crowd was upon us. Visitación shoved them away. I followed her, pushing the wheelbarrow we were using to transport Jesús to the city hall entrance. Consuelo stuck to my side.

"Get back, all of you!"

She grabbed a shovel and brandished it in the air.

Locals and out-of-towners alike parted to let us through, and the city hall guards looked the other way. We headed for Aurelio Ortiz's office.

Visitación barged through the door and proceeded toward the desk, where the mayor was devouring a shredded beef empanada.

"Aurelio Ortiz, you've shut down The Third Country on me!" she shouted, furious.

"It's an administrative precaution." He spoke with his mouth full, cleaning his hands on a crumpled napkin.

"No, m'hijo! That is no precaution: it's an injustice! Angustias, come here!"

Aurelio looked at me, shaking his head. I pushed the wheelbarrow as far as the mayor's desk.

"Don't make me call the police," he threatened.

Jairo appeared with Candelaria on his arm. They were walking as one: he with his accordion on his chest and she, by his side, taking small steps in her black canvas shoes.

"Angustias, help me!" ordered Visitación.

Between the two of us, we lifted the body and placed it on the desk.

"You decide, Aurelio Ortiz. What are you going to do with this dead man? If I can't bury him in The Third Country, he will have to be buried somewhere."

With his eyes fixed on the lifeless body, the mayor vomited.

"Take it out of here at once!" ordered Aurelio Ortiz after wiping his mouth with a handkerchief.

"I can't, sir," answered the police officer.

"If you're so afraid," Aurelio turned around and pointed to the other man in the room, "then Gamboa will do it."

"I'm not touching it either."

Outside, in the hall, the mob tried to force their way in. Nobody wanted to miss the show.

"In that case, throw all these people out of here. Tell them to come back tomorrow, city hall is closed."

The police officers didn't move.

"Gamboa, make it today!" Aurelio was desperate. Nobody was obeying him.

Consuelo fidgeted, wanting to say something.

"Keep your mouth shut." Angustias dug her fingernails into the girl's arm. "Don't stir up more trouble than we already have on our hands."

Aurelio Ortiz looked at the dead body and the trail of papers and mess around him. He couldn't escape his misfortune. It didn't matter what he did.

"You win, Visitación. Two city hall employees will go with you to open the cemetery. But do me a favor and get that body out of here."

That was how Aurelio lifted the mayor's decree on The Third Country and granted a deferral until its definitive closure.

I n town they called him a coward. And Aurelio Ortiz was, but they were mistaken about the reasons.

"You're not getting away with this. Come right away," Abundio growled down the phone.

When he arrived at the hacienda, in the late afternoon, Aurelio found the old man seated on the leather chair that dominated his office. In one hand he held a gun, and in the other hand was a towel dipped in oil, which he was using to polish the firearm until it gleamed.

"Come in, I'm not going to shoot you right now! If you're lucky, and if you've got a good excuse, I'll do it tomorrow." The old man snapped his fingers. "Perpetua, get out of here! Go see if the goose has laid any golden eggs. And leave the phone here, I don't like you going around all day fiddling with that thing."

She placed the device on the desk and left without a word.

"What are you doing here, Aurelio? Come in, I don't have all day!"

Abundio stored the shotgun with his other firearms and turned to pour a whiskey. Aurelio's legs were weak, and his heart was racing. He couldn't tell whether the sound he heard was the chattering of his teeth or the ice clinking in the glass.

"You let an old lady and a dead body fuck you over," Abundio got theatrical. "How could you let Visitación dump a corpse on your desk? And, even worse . . . how did it occur to you to give in to her demands?"

He turned around and looked at Aurelio, the whiskey in hand.

"At this rate, she'll end up in charge." He took a seat without inviting Aurelio to do the same. "It doesn't bother me that you've disobeyed me. What pisses me off is that you let me down." He took a sip. "I don't like disloyal . . ."

Aurelio coughed and lowered his gaze.

"Look me in the eye, for fuck's sake! Be a man! I was clear with you: we are going to close that dump and tear it down. I promised those bones to the irregulars, and you know how they get when people don't keep to their word! Mono is contemplating making a new pair of boots with your hide, Aurelio!" Abundio grew serious. "You have undermined me, and in these circumstances, I find it very difficult to protect you. . . ." He took another gulp. "Or your children. And, if pushed, even your wife." He got up again and filled his glass. "You have no ambition, Aurelio!" He lowered his voice: "Deep down your thing was always that graphing calculator, wasn't it? Stamping documents, working out the figures, balancing accounts for Cucaña storekeepers . . ."

The mayor looked at the cabinet full of guns and for a moment considered grabbing one and blowing Abundio to bits.

"I was mistaken about you. . . ."

Aurelio Ortiz, business administration graduate and county registrar, was in a bind, the only available escape by way of a bullet to the head or vanishing without a trace.

"From this point forward, the guerrillas will be after you, determined to hang your head like a garland from one of the interstate streetlights!" shouted the old man, bringing him back to reality.

It was all the same. If Mono's men didn't kill him, Abundio would stage an ambush with his own. He would send him to Tren del Llano or to any of those henchmen he used to shake down traders all over the mountains. In the towns in the border region, all shadows hid a predator.

"Prohibiting the burial of those dead won't change anything," Aurelio swallowed saliva.

"What did you say?" Abundio pointed to his ear. "Repeat that."

The mayor's mind went blank.

"Repeat it!"

"Closing The Third Country would benefit Visitación, in the long run. People would blame you, not her."

"You are so fucking naive. How do you think things work in Mezquite? People have never loved me, but they are afraid of me, and that's enough." He let out a laugh, flashing his three gold molars. "I'm in charge here! You became mayor thanks to me and the votes I fixed! Not because they wanted you. . . ."

Abundio paused.

"Who is Aurelio Ortiz and who is Alcides Abundio?"

"People have a right to bury their dead . . . ," he stated quietly.

"Careful, or the Black woman will soon be burying you."

He glanced at the wall clock and waved to signal that he should leave his office.

"You are relieved of this, as well as all other matters you carry out for me, including at city hall."

Aurelio retreated, without turning his back on Abundio.

"You can walk normally, Aurelio. I'm not going to shoot you in the back. There are people more willing than I." A flimsy smile crossed his face. "May God protect you, Aurelio. I can't anymore . . . nor do I want to."

The mayor passed through the halls of the mansion with the certainty that it would be the last time he set foot in that place. At the entrance he came across Mercedes. She looked exhausted. She was furious.

"Carmen, come here at once!"

"Wait a sec, Mamá," responded the girl, in the distance.

"I said come *here!*"

"Doña Mercedes, don't be like that, she's only playing. . . ."

"Shut up, Misericordia. She's my daughter!"

Aurelio hid behind a column. Seated on the roots of the sand-paper tree, Carmen was watching Críspulo, who held a stick in one hand and a blade in the other.

"Get away from my daughter!" yelled Mercedes, but Críspulo didn't even look up.

"Mami, Críspulo is going to make me a flute!"

Mercedes slapped her daughter. And slapped her again, and again.

"Don't hit me, Mamita! Críspulo is my friend!"

"Críspulo is not your friend!"

Misericordia placed her hand on Mercedes's shoulder.

"Doña Mercedes, everything is alright."

She spun around, hysterical, her hair all over the place.

"Mind your business and let me mind my own." She grabbed her daughter and dragged her down the hall.

Críspulo finished whittling the flute and placed it on a table in the entranceway; then he put away his knife and walked toward the dog kennel.

Aurelio Ortiz passed through the empty hallway that led to the main door. On the tiled floor he noticed something white and shiny. Thinking it was an earring, he bent down to pick it up.

It was a milk tooth stained with fresh blood.

anging from the sign that read THE THIRD COUNTRY, Críspulo Miranda's German shepherd was bleeding out beneath the midday sun. A cloud of flies hovered over the puddle its blood was forming on the sand. We splashed the dog with kerosene and set fire to it. The smoke smudged the air with a heavy, bleak odor.

We buried Jesús after praying an Our Father. There was no time for anything more elaborate. Jairo stayed behind, with the accordion on his back, and Consuelo waited with Candelaria, who was murmuring prayers under her breath.

Visitación and I churned the cement mix and sealed the grave. It was a race against time. Tolvaneras had become an hourglass, and it was swallowing us alive. From now on, things could only deteriorate. For once in his life Aurelio Ortiz had not been a coward, but in postponing the cemetery's closure he had only given us a head start. Between Abundio's fury and our dead lay The Third Country, a declaration of war. It was a war we were incapable of waging.

We gathered everything and stowed it in the shed. Before leaving, I grabbed two palm-leaf wreaths and took them to where my sons were lying. I tried to arrange them gracefully, but they looked lousy. The burial chamber did too. Graves never changed their appearance. They were immutable. Around my sons' grave, nothing grew, not even grass.

Visitación tooted the horn.

"Angustias, hurry up, we're late!"

When I crouched down to attach the wreaths, I found candies next to the grave.

"If you don't get in right away, I'm leaving you behind!" she shouted.

I collected the candies and ran toward the pickup. Consuelo and Candelaria were traveling with Visitación in the cabin. I made myself comfortable on the bed next to the coplero.

"Jairo, sing something!" shouted Visitación before she turned the key in the ignition.

"Now's not the time for revelries," he responded, covering his face with his cap.

We made for the interstate, which at that time of day was full of hungry goats picking through the trash. The coplero's face had clouded over. He had barely said anything since we left Mezquite. When we passed through a tollbooth, he started talking.

"Your husband?"

"He left."

"I know that. Have you heard from him?"

I shook my head.

"Lots of people say they've seen him."

"How can they recognize somebody they've never spoken to?"

Jairo removed his accordion and stored it beneath a tarp next to the bags of cement.

"Life is not a copla." I leaned on the spare wheel. "Stop talking nonsense. . . ."

"I just want to help you."

"And who told you I wanted help? Do I have a needy face? Have I asked you for help? Focus on your singing and leave me alone!"

He came closer and lowered his voice.

"He's been sighted in several mountain towns. In Tolvaneras too, a few days ago. That man is looking for you. Have you noticed anything strange?"

"He almost killed us a few days ago. Is that strange enough for you?"

"Everyone's talking about that in the mountains. How many of them were there?"

"A lot. I couldn't see their faces. Only hear them. . . ."

"And your husband was among them, was he?"

"Have you been told that too, or did you make it up?"

"People shouted it today at city hall. He's running with them."

"People, people . . . I don't care about people! They never help, never take pity!"

"Is it true what they say? Did you drive them away with snakes?"

"They must have slithered out of the graves. . . ."

"From your sons' grave too, Angustias?"

I took the candies out of my pocket and studied them. They were wrapped in colorful paper.

"Angustias, are you listening?"

"Lay off already, Jairo."

He leaned back. He stretched his arms and legs, looked like a snake sizing up its prey before striking.

"Since he's fallen in with the irregulars, your husband is a dead man. Guys like him don't live long. I, on the other hand, am alive."

In Tolvaneras, the moon seemed more fickle than anywhere else in the border region, but that night it shone like a white disk. Its light bathed Jairo's brown face.

"What's wrong, Angustias? Are you afraid of me? Or do you only have feelings for the dead?"

"I know what to expect from the dead."

The bed shook. The pickup left the tarmac. The impact sent me sailing, and I rolled in the undergrowth. Lying in a ditch, I saw a jeep speeding away.

My mouth tasted like dust, and pain reverberated through my body. Jairo tried to help me out of the ditch, but I could barely move.

"Give her water, Jairo."

"Visitación? Is that you?"

"Who were you expecting, the Virgin Mary?"

Her scarf was still tied around her head, but her leggings were torn.

"What happened?"

"We were run off the road. Are you okay? Does anything hurt?"

He handed me a plastic bottle to drink from. I spat it out straight away.

"That's aguardiente!"

"Drink!" ordered Visitación.

The liquor seared my throat, like anesthetic. First, I recovered movement in my arms, then in my legs, until, gradually, I was able to stand. Jairo observed me attentively, ready to catch me if I fell. He had a bright thread on his forehead. In the moonlight, even blood looked like metal.

"Shhhhhh," warned the coplero. "I can hear a motor revving."

"Everyone get down!" Visitación lay on the ground. "In case they're coming back to finish us off."

"Why don't we cry out for help?" asked Consuelo.

"Lower your voice, you silly girl! Help Candelaria!"

We waited a few minutes, listening to the motor. When it drew away, we sat up again.

"It's leaving," said Visitación. "Its lights are off so we can't see it."

The pickup was stalled in the trench, where it had come to a stop after swerving off the highway. The two front wheels had taken the impact. One had been cut up by the rocks while the other was flat. We had only one spare, but we would still manage.

"When I was in the ditch, I saw a jeep speeding off. What happened?" I asked as I helped Visitación replace the tire.

"A pair of assholes ran us off the road. Jairo, bring me the wrench too. It's next to the spare."

Although she seemed exhausted, Visitación exhibited more energy than usual. First, she removed the wheel nuts and then the studs. She heaved off the damaged tire and placed it to one side. Her movements were swift and barely gave me time to continue my line of questioning.

"The jeep was hurtling toward us, with the lights on high. The lights blinded me, and I lost control, but the sand brought us to a standstill. With Jairo's help, I pulled out Candelaria first, and then Consuelo. You got the worst of it. You went flying into the air."

"What were the men like?"

"Hold the flashlight higher," she ordered. The last stud was difficult to remove. Visitación insisted on doing it herself until it came free. "I don't know." She wiped her forehead with the back of her hand and shined the flashlight on the hub before turning it on my face. "You're bleeding, Angustias."

She undid the knot of her headscarf and removed it. A ponytail of thick hair fell to her waist. Without her headscarf, Visitación seemed younger, an attractive woman entombed in layers of dust and dirt.

"What are you looking at?" She wound the headscarf around my head, handling me roughly. "Quit quizzing me and help!"

Crouched before the spare, which was only halfway on, we heard a siren. It was an ambulance speeding down the highway.

"A turbulent night. Take me home, Visitación," said Candelaria.

"Whatever you say, doña." Visitación stood up. "Hurry up, Jairo! At this rate we won't be leaving until tomorrow."

He tightened the remaining nuts. While they finished up, I walked around. Not far from the pickup I found the accordion. Its bellows was broken, and a few keys were missing. Jairo tried to play it, but he could barely get a note out.

"I don't think it's worth fixing. . . ."

He slung the instrument over his shoulder, whistling. He hopped up onto the pickup and lay back in the bed.

"Jairo. . . . What are you doing, just lounging there? Get down right now!" Visitación relentlessly berated him until he was on his feet again. "Put the flat tire in its place! Do you expect me to do that too? The cheek!"

I stayed where I was, at a remove from the shouting. Only then did I hear the pygmy owl sing once more.

ore than illuminating objects, the moon seemed to flay them. Aurelio Ortiz killed the engine and stepped out of the mayoral jeep hastily. He opened the door to his house and, once inside, double locked it before going to find his wife. She was in bed, about to fall sleep.

"Salvación, we're leaving. Go get the kids, quick!"

He could barely summon the words, but his wife demanded an explanation.

"Just listen to me, and pack whatever you can," he pleaded.

It was useless. She would not lift a finger until he told her what was happening.

"Have you looked at your face in the mirror? You're pale."

"Abundio sacked me. Put any essentials into a suitcase."

"What do you mean, sacked you?!" shrieked his wife, pulling back the sheets. "You're the mayor! You were chosen by the people! You can't leave like this!"

"I'll explain everything when we're on the road."

"I knew it, I knew it, I knew it," she murmured as she headed for the boys' room.

Almost in a trance, and still wearing her cotton nightgown, she got their boys out of bed and started dressing them without turning on the light.

"Arturo, look out for your brother. He's little and he's scared of the dark. Don't cry or shout, set a good example," she told the eldest as she buttoned his trousers.

Aurelio Ortiz pulled a rucksack full of cash out of the bottom drawer: the cut Abundio gave him for the commissions collected in his name. He shoved a pistol he didn't know how to use into the bag too, and the credentials he needed to get through the inspections and checkpoints. He had to be quick. Once news got out, those documents would be worth exactly nothing.

His eldest boy's crying pulled him from his thoughts. Aurelio ran to the room with his index finger on his lips. Any noise would put them in even greater danger. The boy was dazed and cross. The baby was sleeping in his crib. On her knees, Salvación was shoving a packet of diapers into a small bag.

"You should have seen this coming," she reproached him, looking into his eyes.

Aurelio left the room even more nervous. He emptied his pockets, the drawers of the sideboard, and the kitchen cupboard too.

"Salvación, where are the keys to my pickup?"

"Reyes has them."

"You gave them to him?" he asked, pale.

"You asked him to take the pickup to the mechanics, have you forgotten?"

A dark cloud crossed his mind.

"Bad news," he murmured, headed for the living room.

Fleeing was the only thing Aurelio Ortiz was good at. He could still buy time and get a few steps ahead of the old man and his men, but he had to do it now. Once his wife grabbed the boys' things and he got hold of all the cash, they left the house.

"If anybody stops us or searches us, hold on to the boys and don't breathe a word."

Instead of being comforting, his words distressed her further.

"Why are you so afraid, Aurelio? Who else is looking for you?"

"Everybody."

He settled a blanket over her, closed the Corolla door, and got into the driver's seat. Hidden beneath the heavy covering, Salvación cursed the day she decided to marry the most cowardly man in the mountains.

They left the town and gave Tolvaneras a wide berth.

Aurelio's eldest son whimpered, curled up in a ball behind the passenger seat. Salvación had the baby in her arms. She tried to calm him by stroking his head.

The phone sounded. It was Reyes. Aurelio put the device on silent and concentrated in the dark, which was the only sure thing at that hour.

"They haven't found me, they're not going to find me," he repeated, his eyes fixed on the rearview mirror.

Three hundred and seventy miles lay between him and San Fernando de las Salinas. If he managed to leave Mezquite and reach this destination, they would be safe. Before he joined the interstate, he made out the lights of a vehicle stuck in the brush. He turned off his own. God had not made him brave, but may he at least make him invisible. He slowed down and glanced at the clock on the dash. It was twelve, the witching hour.

n the mountains, people believed in apparitions. Roads were dotted with crosses, Madonnas, and small cement altars topped with candles in memory of accident victims, a vigil of guttering flames in the gloom.

The most dangerous curves inspired specters and legends: the woman in white here, the headless man there, the boy ghost, the adolescent who asked to be given a lift to the border. This last one was the most feared. It was said to be the soul in torment of a young man who tried, over and again, to hitch a ride along the stretch of the road he was yet to travel the night he was run over.

So it was in the mountains. The spirits and the living comingled until they formed a crowd of misfortunes that served to scare off the curious and veil the executioners. The spirits were useful. They provided camouflage and made things easy for anyone who did not want to be seen or found.

Fear is a great deterrence. That was the first thing Aurelio learned from Abundio's men. If somebody was driving in the middle of the night, the later the better, they threw an animal at the windshield, or sometimes only a stone. The surprise made the driver lose control, and once they were off the road, disarming and subduing them was a simple matter.

The moans and cries attributed to ghosts sometimes masked executions and beatings. It was as if spirits and ghosts from the afterlife had begun to reign on earth: maybe that sound was the ill-fated bride on the side of the road, or the invisible man who whistled in the dark. All these inventions became a way for guerrillas, traffickers, and snitches to disguise their misdeeds. Even the police spread rumors to cover their own backs.

Aurelio could not tell who had run off the road. He saw only silhouettes, three or four shadows blurred in the moonlight. He slowed further. So long as the sky remained clear, the brightness meant he could get his bearings and react quickly to any ambush. If he could remain hidden, he would be safe.

Whoever it was would have to hope that either God would help them or that the executioner, if there was one, would come back to put them out of their misery. That was the way it went on the border, and there was little he could do to change it. If he hadn't been able to change it as mayor, he had no chance of doing so as a fugitive. He looked behind him. His wife and sons were sleeping beneath the blanket. *May each of us deal with death as best we can*, he thought, his hands gripping on the wheel.

Draped as it was in a dark burial shroud, the landscape looked different, but he knew the road, and that gave him confidence. He had traveled it hundreds of times, the first more than twenty years ago, when he left Mezquite to study in the capital. That day, his father hadn't come to say goodbye, offended that he had turned down an opportunity to study teaching. His father still didn't understand, and perhaps never would, but Aurelio was not like him. He did not want to teach, did not aspire to gaining anyone's respect, only desired a better life: to have a big house, a position in the local government, protection from the powerful, or—why not?—to be one of them.

When he returned with a university degree under his arm, his old man lost his head. His father had withstood the assaults that time and life had delivered, blow after blow, including the death of his wife and bringing up a boy in whom he never saw any signs of promise. Or at least he never let Aurelio know of any he appreciated. He never said anything encouraging while he was sane, so there was no chance of him doing so now that Alzheimer's had swarmed him with ghosts.

While Aurelio reviewed his own specters, an ambulance flew by toward Mezquite. Only somebody with a lot of money could afford to engage one. With his eyes fixed on the rearview mirror, Aurelio Ortiz saw the red and blue lights move away. Something terrible must have happened in town.

The sky was clear and desolate. The breeze barely blew, and the moon seemed to expand, hungry, in the middle of the darkness. My head was buzzing, and my back felt pommeled. I sat next to Consuelo while Visitación helped Candelaria into the cabin, so she could rest before we left.

"So you came back to Mezquite. . . ."

"A few months ago. . . ."

"Why didn't you come find me?"

She shrugged.

"And what about that belly?"

"Angustias! Ten more minutes and we're out of here!" shouted Visitación. "Leave the chitchat for later!"

"What's with that lady?" Consuelo sulked. "She only ever treats me bad. It's not like I've done anything to her."

"You know her. You know how she can be."

"Nah. I've always treated her right, I was always sent to fetch her when somebody died. . . ."

"Did you really work in a dive bar?"

"Not anymore. The owner made my life impossible."

Visitación and Jairo stowed the tools.

"Enough talk! We're out of here! Hey preggers, you get in and help Candelaria!" Visitación's hands were covered in engine grease. "Angustias, you in the back, with the poet . . ."

I climbed into the bed and held out my hand.

"Can you manage it yourself, or do you need some help?"

"Do me a favor and let's travel what remains of this trip in peace," he answered, annoyed.

"Whatever you say, Jairo."

We said not another word to each other for the rest of the trip.

After Nopales, we kept on toward Mezquite. The night had retreated, as if the birdsong had brought on daybreak. Mezquite's streets were deserted and emptied of people, a haze of ash the only thing moving, and on the facade of city hall, three black Xs still dripped fresh paint.

"The irregulars have been through here."

Visitación motioned to the painted Xs with her lips, annoyed. At this time of day, stallholders were usually unloading their goods, but we only found closed doors and lowered shutters. Not even coffee steam was appearing on kitchen windows.

Nobody would open for us at the clinic. We persisted until a woman spoke to us without unlatching the door.

"Where's the doctor?" Visitación didn't even say good morning.

"He arrives at eight."

"We'll wait for him then."

"Up to you." And she shut the door without a further word.

We waited more than an hour and a half. A tall, dark man appeared with the keys in hand and motioned for us to follow. He seemed pinched, as if he had not slept.

"Are you the doctor?" Visitación was the first to speak.

The man nodded, not even saying his name.

"Last night we had an accident on the highway."

"There were several yesterday," he answered, adjusting his white coat.

"Can you examine her first?" I pointed at Consuelo. "She's pregnant, and we want to know if the knock . . ."

"You have a wound on your forehead. It's a big one."

"But she . . ."

"Take a seat."

He turned around and rummaged in the cabinet.

"There's no suture thread!"

The woman who had spoken to us earlier came into the consulting room with a bucket of water in hand.

"What's wrong?"

"There's not enough of this! I can't suture with it!"

"It's all that's left."

The doctor's hair was poorly cut, and he wore a faded shirt beneath his white coat. He was not old, but not young either. If it had not been for his stethoscope, I would have thought he was a security guard or a janitor.

"This is going to hurt."

He sank the needle into my skin, piercing it like a piece of fabric. He repeated the motion four or five times until he had brought together the flaps of skin on both sides of the wound. I stood, black sutures marking my forehead. The skin felt tight and stung. I left the examination table free for Consuelo, who got up grudgingly. The doctor checked her over slowly, feeling her arms and legs, then her stomach.

"Does this hurt? And here? No? Are you sure?"

He wanted to know if she had felt anything after the accident, but she only described giddiness and aches, vague remarks that were not convincing.

"You have three bruises on your legs. But there are no fractures or hemorrhaging. How far along are you?"

"I don't know."

"Is a doctor monitoring your progress?"

She shook her head.

"Did you have any bleeding after the impact?"

She shrugged her shoulders.

"Did you bleed or not?"

She shook her head again.

"The fetus seems okay, but I can't guarantee it." He jotted something down on a blank page.

Visitación pulled out her handkerchief and wiped the sweat from her forehead.

"What's your name?"

"Consuelo Matute."

"How old are you?"

"Fifteen, my birthday was yesterday."

The doctor told her to get on the scale. Fifty kilos, and five feet two. A bag of bones held together by tattered clothing.

"Do you have any family?"

"An aunt in the eastern mountains."

The heat was unbearable. He opened the only window overlooking the street so that air might circulate, then gave her a final look over.

"You can get up," he said. "Now it's your turn."

Visitación adjusted her leggings with both hands and then put her hands on her hips. Two beads of sweat were forming beneath her armpits.

"Stretch out your arm."

"What's happening in this town?" she asked.

"If you speak, I can't take your blood pressure. Be quiet, please."

He pressed the button until the cuff was fully inflated. He checked her blood pressure and noted the number on another page.

"You're not going to answer me?"

"Concerning?"

"Concerning what I asked you."

"I'm here to attend to patients."

Visitación let him examine her, displeased.

"Can I speak now?"

"Have you had heart palpitations?"

"Never!"

"Do you exercise?"

"A lot, especially at night, and always in company."

"Do you walk? Lift weights?"

"All of that at once. I also smoke, drink, and party." The doctor loosened the device.

"You don't seem to be in shape, you have high blood pressure."

He rummaged in the desk, grabbed a booklet, and scribbled instructions on the paper.

"This is for you to get an ultrasound at Cucaña hospital." He handed the referral to Consuelo. "Go there tomorrow."

She folded the slip of paper and tucked it into her rucksack. She was covered in dust, thorns still stuck to her clothing.

"And you," he said to me, "apply this twice a day, after bathing the wound in water and soap. It's an antiseptic."

Visitación took one step forward and lifted her index finger, ready to say something.

"As far as I'm concerned, there is nothing more to be said."

"But . . ."

"Good day," said the doctor.

Visitación was still mumbling expletives about the doctor. He had not even examined her properly, she was saying. She didn't direct a word to us until we arrived at the market stalls, where a group of men and women were huddled by the eating area. They were talking about an ambulance. Perhaps the priest had been whisked away in it, his stomach full of coins. Perhaps Abundio had been inside, his wife with him. Perhaps there had been a shoot-out at the hacienda.

One of the stallholders looked at us, debating whether to come over.

"I'm sorry about Víctor Hugo."

Visitación rolled her eyes.

"What happened? Has he been arrested?"

The stallholder swayed a little, as if he wanted to back up.

"Come on, tell me!"

"He and the mayor's drivers were executed. You know, the ones in uniform."

We also discovered that Aurelio Ortiz had left town with his family. The stallholder said nothing about the black crosses on the facade of city hall. We all knew what they meant.

As much as she tried to hide it, the news left Visitación in low spirits.

We piled into the pickup and drove to the marketplace garages, but nobody wanted to sell us any gasoline. The same with food. The poultry seller had no eggs, the baker no change, the fruit seller had stepped out. Even the Lebanese bar owner refused to sell us three bottles of water.

"To take with you, but not to have here."

"What's going on? Now we can't come in?"

The man looked around and lowered his voice.

"People are nervous. Listen to what I'm telling you, come back some other day."

The three of us were left standing at the bar, not sure what to do.

"All because of you, Visitación!" let fly a kiosk owner.

"You and your dead need to get out of here!" added the baker.

"I don't want any trouble," begged the bar owner. "If I serve you anything, I'll be crucified. Just leave, please."

When we got to the main square, we found the pickup's four tires slashed. The war had begun.

urelio Ortiz stopped at a gas station. There were still sixty miles between him and the coast, and he now had less than a quarter tank of gasoline. The boys were hungry, and his back was killing him. After refueling, he parked next to the stalls where fishermen sold shellfish with salt and lemon.

He was going to call Reyes from a grocery store that had a pay phone, but he stopped himself. Instead, he bought a packet of soda crackers, a bunch of bananas, and three bottles of water. His wife peeled some of the fruit and gave half to her eldest. She drank some water and unbuttoned her shirt to feed the baby. Aurelio sat down next to her, ready to tell her everything, but she cut him off.

"What are we going to do?" she asked, her hand around one breast.

"For the time being, we'll go to your sister's house. We've passed through three checkpoints, and so far, they've accepted the three names I've given."

"Arturo, leave that! Come back here!"

Their eldest was playing on rusty swings. Aurelio looked at Salvación's dark nipple, which their other son latched onto greedily.

"Arturo, get down from there right now!" she repeated.

She covered herself up and, with the baby still in her arms, walked over to the playground, which was being eaten up by salt residue. She grabbed her eldest son and dragged him away by the hand. Aurelio made as if to hug her.

"Don't come near me."

Planted in pots around the square, sea grape trees swayed in the warm, salty breeze. The nearness of the sea had altered everything:

the temperature, the landscape, even the light. Unlike Mezquite, no walkers found their way to the coast, nor black marketers, and few criminals.

Salvación rummaged around in her bag. She removed her phone and, in a precarious balancing act, pressed the screen with her thumb.

"What are you doing?" Aurelio pounced on her. "Turn that off!"

Annoyed, she handed him the baby.

"Could you take care of the boys while I call my sister from a pay phone? Or do you need an assistant for that?"

She grabbed the cloth she had used to cover herself and placed it on Aurelio's shoulder.

"If he cries, rock him facedown, so he sleeps. If he keeps crying, sniff his diaper."

She made for the restroom, swaying her hips.

Aurelio was about to explode. His anger outweighed his exhaustion. He hadn't showered for two days, and a greasy film was covering his face. His linen trousers had turned into a limp rag, as had his political career.

Seated on a metal bench, he waited with the baby in his arms while his eldest son played with a tamarind pod. Two Wayuu women dressed in colorful dresses passed by. Half their faces were covered in black paint. Whenever his father took him to the coast to eat rice and coconut, he would see them crossing the road. He would be dumbstruck by their distant, sullen beauty. They would be walking, as they did now, carrying woven hammocks and baskets to peddle.

Much was said about the Wayuu—that they were mistrustful, for example—but Aurelio never believed the tales. Like everyone else, they did whatever was needed to get by. Everyone did what they could with their lot, he thought, looking at the women. He found them just as beautiful now, maybe even more so, than back in the days when his father did his best to show his affection.

"Look, Aurelio, there go the Wayuu princesses," he would say amid the food vapors and humidity of the coast.

"What's a Wayuu?"

"They're people who live on the border, between the sea and the earth, the desert and the water. They walk the line between life and death."

The reverie didn't last long. The baby erupted into screams and turned red. Aurelio held the cloth to him, rocked him face-down, gave him a little water, but nothing worked. Only then did he realize he had never held him for more than a few minutes at a time.

Salvación appeared, her hair damp and her face freshly washed.

"I spoke to my sister. I told her we would be there in two hours." She took the baby into her arms.

"Did you tell her anything?"

"I pretended we wanted to give her a surprise, but she didn't believe me. . . . Arturo, let that go!"

She snatched away the tamarind pod and came back to her husband.

"Salvación, let me explain. . . ."

"I don't want to know anything. Give me the keys."

"What for?"

"You take care of the boys. I'm driving."

She got into the Corolla, put her foot on the clutch, and started the engine. Aurelio made himself comfortable in the back seat with the boys. His eldest son snuggled into him, clenching the blanket.

"Can you hide me, Papá?"

"That game's over, Arturo. Sleep. When you wake up, we'll go have a dip in the sea."

"What's the sea?"

"It's like a big river, but salty."

Aurelio noticed his wife scrutinizing him in the rearview mirror.

"We could have avoided this, Aurelio," she said, gritting her teeth.

Salvación stepped on the accelerator and took off without looking back.

Outside, the Wayuu women were making their way toward the bay in their colorful clothing, their almond eyes peeping out from polish-smeared faces. Aurelio clicked his tongue. Not even the princesses of his childhood could save him now.

Her daughters barely let her get a word in. All over the mountains, different versions of what had happened at city hall were circulating, and although Visitación tried to convince them that the tales were exaggerations, they wouldn't believe her. They were right not to.

"Mamá, quit stirring up trouble and come home!"

"I've raised four children and buried two. You're not going to order me around."

With her scarf tied around her head once more, Visitación had regained her authority.

"Whatever you say goes, Mamá, but . . ."

"Take me to Cucaña. I need four new tires, they've all been slashed."

"She's lost her mind!" the youngest blew up.

"Shut up, Jennifer!" her sister ordered. "Listen, Mamá, we'll buy the replacements, but afterward you're coming with us for a few days. People are saying Abundio has been killed!"

"And that the mayor fled," chimed in the other.

"I'm not leaving my dead!"

"Well, we're alive, and we have something to say too, Mamá! You're so stubborn!"

They interrupted each other, like always.

"Alright, alright!" I shouted.

Visitación froze.

"Fuel to the fire!" she let out. "And what's got into you? Why are you shouting?"

"Does that cemetery mean so much to you that you won't listen to your own flesh and blood?"

"Have some respect, Angustias!" she retorted. "Mind your own business."

"Go stay with them for a few weeks. Lots of strange people are hanging around Tolvaneras, and things are getting ugly."

"That's nothing new," she remarked, downplaying my words. "They've always wanted to frighten us. And they've never managed to."

"Until, instead of fear, they put a bullet in you!"

"What would you know!" She raised her hand to give Jennifer a slap on the neck, but Jennifer was quicker and ducked out of the way.

"This time's different, Visitación," I insisted. "Somebody leaves things for my sons. Wooden figurines and candies. There is never anything on any other grave, only on my twins'. I don't know if it's Salveiro or someone else."

"Talkalot? Your husband? But he left here fuming and out of his mind!"

"Jairo says people have sighted him. He said he's taken up with the irregulars."

"That man, a guerrilla?" She let out a laugh. "More likely he's in a mental ward. . . ."

"It was shouted to us in town, but you don't remember. . . ."

"That's sheer fancy!"

"Listen to me, Visitación. Go for a few days," I begged, not holding out much hope.

"Listen to what Angustias is telling you, Mamá!" the other two insisted.

"Shut up, for God's sake! What a cowardly lot you are! Diddums, you poor little damsels. That's what you are: sulky damsels."

Her daughters and I looked at one another.

"Well, since you're so scared, we'll all leave this place. But on one condition: we come back in three days."

I nodded.

"You go with Consuelo," I said, "I'll stay at the cemetery."

"I've never been one to hold anything back, so I'll say it nice and clear: I don't trust that girl."

Consuelo pulled a face while Visitación sounded off.

"I've seen her go from family to family, first hanging on to one, then switching to another, she looks after so-and-so's children, then what's-his-name's, she shacks up with the cousins or uncles. Did somebody from Cuchillo Blanco give you that belly?"

"You don't know me. You know nothing about me." Consuelo pressed her lips together.

"I know nothing? Then how come you tired yourself out coming to find me to bury people? I've had my eye on you, and it's been that way for a long time."

"Well if you don't want to take me, then I don't want to go with you."

Visitación snorted.

"Angustias Romero, you're so stubborn! The problems this girl could bring us, and you insist! I'm telling you she's not squeaky clean, far from it."

"Víctor Hugo, the boyfriend you thought was dopey, gave us more trouble."

"Oh come on, Angustias. . . ." Visitación passed her hand over her mouth. "Look, it's all the same to me. I've only got myself. That's always been glaringly clear."

"If you know how to take care of yourself, then I do too."

She mopped her forehead with her handkerchief and laid out the plan as if she were a sergeant: she would take us to the cemetery after buying the replacement tires. She would be gone three days, long enough to get her thoughts in order and give some time for things to cool.

"On the third day, like Our Lord, I will be back."

She got into her daughters' pickup truck, griping.

"It's an oven in here! Get a good grip of the steering wheel! You're no daughters of mine! What terrible drivers! Straighten your back, Jennifer!"

They left bickering. Consuelo lay down in the cabin; at least she would have some shade while we waited for them to return. I took out one of the cigarettes Visitación kept in the glove box. Seated on the pavement, I watched Visitación and her daughters grow smaller. I lit up the cigarette and smoked half-heartedly, convinced that the next burial I attended would be my own.

A cloud of bumblebees and blowflies were flying around The Third Country. They were fat, heavy insects, black as the seeds of the bay cedar. They looked like stones covered in thistles. Sometimes they would get tangled in our hair, trapped in a knot of strands and sweat, and we would have to pull hard to get them out.

"Get inside, Consuelo. There are bugs."

"I still have to sweep the porch."

"Put down that broom and get under cover."

I had to boil water in a pot before I could tend to my wound. When it was ready, I filtered enough coffee for the both of us, and set aside a portion to wash my scar. My forehead was tense.

"Tomorrow, when Visitación arrives, we'll go to Cucaña."

"I'm not in a hurry. I feel good."

"That's for your doctor to decide, not you."

A storm rumbled in the distance, and the smell of damp earth permeated Tolvaneras. When I went inside the shed, I locked the door behind me and lit a mosquito coil. The smell would be enough to fend off the bugs.

"Drink this coffee. I have to take care of you: you're still the Queen of Mezquite," I laughed, imitating Visitación.

"You're not quite pulling it off. . . . You need a headscarf." She mimicked the posture Visitación adopted when she was being bossy.

"Why does she have it in for me?"

"Ask her . . . , 'you shoe-wearing donkey!'"

We both let out a laugh.

Consuelo occasionally still showed glimpses of the flair she had when I met her. Maybe back then she was already shot through with sorrow and I just hadn't realized.

"I don't have anything against Visitación . . . but she has something against me." She picked up the mug and lay back.

I bathed my wound and cut a piece of thread that the doctor had left sticking from one of the sutures. It looked like a cockroach antenna. The light wasn't great, but at least I could make out the scar . . . and Consuelo's silhouette, which reflected in the mirror.

"How did your parents die?" Not much rubbing alcohol was left, only enough to soak a piece of gauze.

"They drowned while trying to cross the Cumboto."

I left the bottle next to the antiseptic.

"I used to see you with a slacker, he seemed to follow you around everywhere."

"He was the uncle in the last family I lived with."

"How many other families were there?" The stitches looked like rivets, my forehead was going to be left in tatters.

"Five."

"Why so many?"

"After my parents died, I stuck with whichever group I could. It was safer than going around alone. They let me stick with them if I looked after their children, carried their bags, or scavenged things for them."

"It's one thing to go around in a group. . . ." I pressed an alcohol-soaked cotton bud against the wound, "and another to go with a maniac like him. . . . Owwww!"

"Is it burning?"

"No! I'm complaining because I like it! But don't worry, for once you're telling me something about your . . ."

"Let me help. . . ."

"I can do it myself."

When I opened the antiseptic bottle, the plastic applicator slipped.

"And then what happened?"

"What always does. In every family there's a handsy or abusive guy, but this one was different. He sought me out all the time. In the shelters he would get up close, breathe all over my neck. He always found me."

"And you, strong as you are, did you let him?" It was hard to fit the applicator back onto the bottle.

"He threatened me, said he would report me to the police if I didn't sleep with him."

I dabbed the ointment on my stitches. The burning was unbearable.

"Let me. When someone else applies it, it's over before you know it, and it hurts less."

I nodded.

"In the beginning . . ." She moistened the sutures with the rest of the antiseptic. "Does that hurt?"

"Don't stop, don't stop. It will be over sooner, that way. And what happened then with him?"

"Well, what else. I had to do it. . . . In the beginning it didn't happen all that often, but then he wanted to do it all the time."

"Did you do it bareback? Without a condom or any protection?" She feigned deafness as she dabbed the final suture. "What's his name?"

"Ramiro . . ."

"Ramiro what?"

"Is that alright, or should I apply some more?"

"It's fine the way it is." I gathered up the cotton swabs. "I'll be back. I'll just go burn this and turn off the generator."

A cloud was completely covering the sky. It wasn't just the water or air pushing it, but something larger, and purposeless. The wind gives no explanations, and that's why nobody asks it for any, so why did I have to ask Consuelo for hers? I had my reasons for coming here, everyone did. The end of the world had no fixed place, and it meant something different to each of us fleeing it.

Consuelo had adapted to this life as best she could, or so she said. She also said she had no siblings, and that until they crossed the border her parents had made a living selling goods in a store on the main street of Cocuyo, the last city in the eastern mountains.

"I helped out sometimes, but they didn't like me to be in the store. . . ."

She moved her hands to her belly, as if she were afraid that whatever was in there might try to escape.

"The irregulars kidnapped and killed more and more people. Soon my parents were having trouble importing goods to sell, and even when they did, people weren't buying them. Then the plague arrived."

The repellent had burned itself out. On the floor, specks of ash were all that remained next to the bottle where I had set the coil.

"My father insisted on avoiding all checkpoints and following the shortcuts and hidden gullies. It was dangerous, and he knew it."

At the Marraneros Crossing, the first place where the Cumboto intersected the border, the water had snapped the rope people would cling to while they crossed. Despite the rain, her father insisted.

"It was dangerous, and he knew it," she repeated.

The current returned her to the bank where they had started, but her parents were dragged away in seconds.

"The logs and rocks that were carried along by the water pushed them downriver. I saw it happen but couldn't do anything." She took a sip of coffee. "Civil Defense found me the next day. But it was an illegal route and I'd lost my papers, so they took me to the police."

Consuelo spoke as if all of this had happened to another person. Maybe it had stopped mattering to her because she had repeated it so many times in her head. She made a statement to the border guards, who took her to the tents where others were searching for family members. Her uncle and aunt, who were going to take her and her parents in, had died in a kidnapping, she was told before she was taken to a children's shelter.

"I didn't last more than a year. I escaped and got by in the regular shelters; at least there I found other people who were trying to make the crossing."

She followed them from town to town.

"Twice I was left behind. The same was done to the elderly: their family would abandon them at a camp before pushing ahead."

Her mug was empty.

"And what happened with your last family, the one with Ramiro?"

"That was a big group, ten or twelve, but half of them drowned trying to make the river crossing. Ramiro got bossy and the problems started. Do this, do that, carry this, carry that. The more he drank, the worse he got."

"Why didn't you report him? Visitación could have helped you."

"What could I have asked her? I didn't have papers. If I'd said anything, I would have been sent to a checkpoint. When I told him I hadn't got my period, Ramiro said I was stealing from him, that I slept with others secretly. . . . With the money you gave me, I bought a ticket to Mezquite. I found work cleaning the bathrooms of dive bars. At least they let me sleep in the storerooms."

A bang rattled the shed door. I grabbed the machete and brought my finger to my lips. We waited a few minutes in silence.

"Shhhh." I lowered my voice. "Don't move."

I peered out the window but saw no one. When I opened it up, I found blowflies twisting in a tangle above the concrete. I loaded the shotgun.

"Take this." I left her the machete. "If you hear anything strange, hide in the vent, under the trough."

"I'm coming with you."

"Listen to me!" I opened the grate. "Get in!" But she refused.

I didn't come across anything strange, just the same wind and the same plague. I walked over to Higinio and Salustio's grave. Nothing was out of place. I returned to the shed, not making a sound. I locked the door and lay down next to Consuelo, keeping the machete and the shotgun close to each side of the sleeping mat. A flash of lightning lit up the night. Before the thunder could sound, fat drops of rain hit the tin roof.

"Is somebody there?" she asked.

"Nobody. It's the rain." Another lightning strike split the sky. "You didn't answer me," I insisted. "What was that man's full name?"

"Ramiro . . ."

"Ramiro what?"

"Ramiro Nasario, he's from the eastern mountains too. . . ."

It was raining buckets.

"Is he alive?"

"I hope not. I wish the current had taken him too. Then I wouldn't be stuck with this problem."

She rubbed her belly again.

"Those of us from the eastern mountains always bring problems with us . . . ," I murmured.

"Are you going to tell Visitación?"

"Sleep now, tomorrow is a new day."

Outside, the gale was lashing, and the rain flooded the sand, forming puddles.

I walked over to the window and secured the mosquito screen. As I braced it with the pliers, I made out a black silhouette, the shadow of a man in the middle of the storm, moving away.

Aurelio set aside part of the money and opened a bank account in his wife's name to deposit the rest. They settled into the family house where Salvación had grown up, which sat on a large parcel of land by the beach. San Fernando was a safe place, but they were careful not to be seen around town. His sister-in-law was very sharp, and he could think of no convincing means of justifying such a long stay.

Every day he went to the beach with his eldest son to collect guacucos, little clams the current spat onto the shore. They spent all morning collecting them, their knees in the sand. Arturo took it so seriously that he would forget to ask when they were going home or why his mother was so upset. When they arrived back at the house, they washed them under running water and cooked them in a frying pan until the heat of the Teflon forced them open.

"This one's bad!" his son remarked.

"They're not bad, Arturo. If they don't open, we can't eat them. That's all."

"Exactly . . . they're bad!"

"They're off, but they're not bad."

His sister-in-law, who was hanging the laundry in the courtyard, listened to them argue.

"The boy's right. With guacucos, it's the same as with people: some are good and some are bad, but we don't have to put people in a hot pan to know it, do we, Aurelio?"

She wasn't the only one treating him like an intruder. His

wife barely looked at him. Her fury even separated them in bed. The baby slept in a small crib, and the eldest, snug between them, like a wall. The nights were long. The mosquitoes and the heat kept Aurelio wide awake. Whenever he did manage to fall asleep, he woke with a start.

He was obsessed with the image of the dead man on his desk, and the sound of the ambulance headed for town. Visitación and Angustias also haunted his sleepless nights. He thought about turning on his old phone, but he stopped himself. He was afraid it could be traced. Abundio was capable of anything.

No news from the mountains reached the coast, and the two or three nearby stores barely stocked national newspapers. The internet was slow, but even when it was working he failed to find any news in the local papers.

After thinking about it a good while, he introduced himself down at the town garage, a workshop where fishermen took their fishing-boat motors to be repaired. In the door of the premises was parked a large pickup, with space to carry loads and good wheels for navigating difficult terrain.

The owner said he wouldn't look at the Corolla, he only repaired small boats. Aurelio placed five five-hundred-dollar bills on the counter.

"If as well as giving the car a service you lend me your pickup for a few days, I'll give you two hundred more."

"Is the Corolla yours?" the man asked.

"The ownership documents are in the glove box, you can take a look at them. Your pickup is legal too, isn't it?"

He nodded.

"Here on the coast, people are respectable, and we expect others to be too."

"Good thing you do," answered Aurelio uncomfortably.

After counting the money, the man took out a booklet, jotted down the total, and gave the page to Aurelio, who used his wife's surname and signed with a scrawl. To cover his back, he added a five-hundred-dollar bill that wasn't recorded on the piece of paper.

"Hold the Corolla as a guarantee, in case I'm a little longer than expected."

"I've never seen you around here."

"I'm the Rodríguezes' son-in-law. They live next door."

The mechanic was not completely convinced, but the bills were enough to persuade him. Aurelio returned home driving the pickup. His wife hadn't spoken to him all morning, but when she saw him, she started with her questions. "Whose pickup is that?" "Where are you going?" "You're not going to dump us here and leave, are you?" "Explain yourself, I have a right to know!"

He remained silent.

"Answer me, Aurelio!"

"If there's an emergency and you need the Corolla, you can go collect it from the mechanic, tell him you're my wife. He will know what to do."

"Don't play deaf with me. You heard me, now answer me."

"Call me if anything bad happens. Use the new phone, but only if it's urgent."

"What are you going to do?"

"Once I'm gone, tell your sister what went down in Mezquite. Don't give too many details. And if anybody asks after me, pretend you have no idea."

"Are you coming back?"

Not even Aurelio was sure of the answer.

"Tell your sister I took some of her husband's clothes," he answered.

He kissed her on the cheek and left the house without making a noise. When he opened the pickup door, he heard his name. It was his son Arturo. He was waiting for him in the doorway with a metal bucket between his hands.

Visitación brought sweet bread and milk for breakfast. She picked her way to the shed in sandals, her pearly painted toenails peeking out.

Her feet were covered in mud. The storm had drowned everything.

After finishing off the bread dipped in milky coffee, we left for Cucaña. The cold early-morning air made us get a move on. Visitación turned on the radio and changed channels until she found one she liked. She left it on a while, and before long was singing.

Bird shit splattered on the windshield.

"Ayyyyyyy fucking pigeon!" She laughed. "Even the Holy Spirit is traveling with us. Look, Angustias! It's a blessing!"

She turned on the windshield wipers while Consuelo murmured a Hail Mary.

My deaf mother and widowed father believed in neither God nor partying, if I'm anything to go by: I rarely think about God, and when I do it's to blame him for things; I think about partying even less, but I find it more bearable than prayers.

When we arrived at Cucaña, I expected the worst: that somebody would open fire on us, or that Consuelo would bump into Ramiro. At the end of the day, it wasn't a big city. We parked near two large containers. Nobody would see the pickup there, and we could slip between the garbage trucks and scrapyard without being seen.

People had formed a line, waiting their turn to go inside the hospital. After two hours, we were finally able to present Consuelo's referral at the information desk. Everything took an age in that place. It was full of women who had traveled there from the eastern mountains to give birth.

When her name was called out, Consuelo jumped to her feet. A nurse approached us.

"Are you her mother?"

"God help us!" Not even then did Visitación let down her guard. "She's the mother."

I got up too.

"Not now. Wait to be called. You, come with me."

Consuelo dragged her feet, as if her shoes stuck to the ground.

"You worry about her too much. She doesn't need to be looked after, she knows more than you and me put together."

"Alright, alright, doña. Enough."

Three other women passed by. Their faces were pinched, their eyes sunken, and they were so skinny their bellies looked like cushions hidden beneath their bones, as if their children devoured them from the inside.

Visitación, who could not bear the silence, started talking about what the gossip was in Mezquite.

"Abundio's house has a black ribbon on the door."

"Did you go there?"

"As if I would, considering the irregulars blew their way onto the hacienda?! I'm telling you what people are saying."

"And who did they kill?"

"I'm not clear whether Abundio, his wife, or their daughter. None of them have been seen for a few days."

"And Críspulo?"

"Holed up somewhere no doubt, all rotters like him are cowards." Visitación turned around in the chair. "And he was right, that stallholder the other day: Aurelio did disappear. He took his family and locked the door behind them. He didn't even pack up his office at city hall."

A bad feeling spread through me. Things were not good, we knew that already. The question was: How much worse could they get?

"Have you gone back to your house in Mezquite?"

She shook her head.

"As if I would go home! The irregulars are on the loose, and they're on a rampage. They already killed Reyes and Víctor Hugo, so they would make ground meat of me." She lowered her voice. "That's the way they work."

A doctor appeared in the corridor. I sat up straight, but he kept on past us.

"And how did you know about Abundio and city hall?" I didn't care, not really, but at least this way the wait would pass quicker.

"Jairo told me."

We both fixed our eyes on a poster with instructions to keep quiet.

"Last night a man came to the cemetery."

"What did he want?"

"I don't know. He did one lap and left."

"Here you go again. Do you really think Talkalot is a guerrilla and wants to do something to us? There's no reason for it to be him. . . ."

"Remember the day the irregulars came?"

"What could you possibly know after that? We couldn't see anything."

"There was one from the eastern mountains. The one who came in all the time. . . ."

"It could have been anyone. It's not as if your husband is the only man who has crossed the border."

"And the toys and candies? And the carved figurines? He was good at working wood."

"He could have left them without being a guerrilla. Maybe he works with the goatherds and shepherds who burn trash?"

Another pregnant woman passed in front of us. Her ankles were swollen, and she had an exhausted expression on her face.

"Will you come back to The Third Country?" I changed the subject.

"Where else would you have me be?"

"With your family and grandchildren. You would be safer with them."

"And my dead, what would happen to them?"

"They will stay in their graves, Visitación. They're never coming out."

A baby floated in the center of the monitor. Its eyes and fists were closed. It was swimming in a sac of water, so content in its cave of blood and flesh. Consuelo didn't even look at it, as if that life weren't hers either.

I stepped away to allow the doctor, a tall, young man, through.

"Are you her mother?" I nodded. "The fetus is healthy, we will see it in more detail now. Come closer." He rubbed the probe across her belly. "Her due date is in one week. She seems to be clear about everything, she hasn't asked any questions." He adjusted his gloves. "And what about you, is there anything you would like to know?"

"I've just come to keep her company."

The doctor dispelled the silence with a few instructions: nutrition, breathing exercises, and sleep habits.

"Where will you give birth, here or in the eastern mountains?" The doctor tried to be warm.

Consuelo didn't bother to answer. I realized time was getting on.

"Mezquite only has one clinic," the doctor continued. "Do you know you can give birth in any hospital in the mountains? You would be taken in here, for example. You just need to show some ID."

"If it's so easy, why are there so many women waiting outside?" was her only question.

"They're not all here for the same thing," he clarified. "Some are here for an ultrasound, like you. Others for monitoring. Many are here to give birth, but not all."

The baby looked larger on the screen. Preoccupied with the dead, I had forgotten how long it takes a life to come into the world.

"Are you sure you're alright, Consuelo?" the doctor tried once more. "Aside from the highway accident, is there anything else? Any physical or mental conditions? Do you sleep well and regularly? Were you taking any medication before you fell pregnant?"

"I've always been very healthy," she said.

"Alright then. In that case, if neither of you has further questions, we're all done here."

"I have a question," I interrupted. "I want to know the sex."

Consuelo turned her face toward the doctor.

"It's a girl."

A voice called from the corridor. The gynecologist left the consulting room and returned a few minutes later with a piece of paper in hand.

"What will you call her? Consuelo is a beautiful name." When he saw that she was not going to answer, he looked over the ultrasound and slipped it into an envelope, noted the date on the back, and scribbled a phone number next to the hospital letterhead. "This is my number. Call me if you have any concerns."

Consuelo cleaned herself off with a tissue and left the consulting room without saying goodbye.

Visitación was watching them through the glass. The neonatal nursery was a bright room covered in white tiles. Nurses were entering and exiting with babies in their arms. Inside, the babies were asleep, wrapped in colorful blankets, and wearing mittens and cotton booties. All of them shared reddened complexions and closed eyes, that squashed look that briefly lingers after they struggle their way into the world.

"What's wrong? You look like you've come straight from a funeral."

Consuelo didn't even look at the babies, only headed for the stairs.

"Give her time for her feelings to settle."

"She doesn't look very happy to me."

"Leave her be. You're always ragging on her."

"What? I just wanted to know how it went! I'll put her straight!"

I took her arm, but she pulled it away.

"Let me go, dammit!"

"Lower your voice, Visitación! Can't you shut your mouth for once?"

"What did I say? Only the truth! She doesn't seem too happy about giving birth."

"You don't understand."

"I understand more than you do, and that's why I'm speaking my mind."

Two doctors looked at us out of the corners of their eyes.

"She's not your family, and her child's not your family either," she whispered. "If she wants to throw that baby into a dumpster, you can't be the one to stop her."

"You can't stand her, I've got that clear." I took a breath. "Sometimes I think you prefer your dead because they can't disagree with you. That's it, isn't it?"

Visitación stormed off. I didn't chase after her. If she and Consuelo were so eager to leave, then they could both go. One to her cemetery, and the other to wherever she felt like.

The nurses' shift change had transformed the corridor into a hubbub of laughter, pranks, and snippets of conversation floating in the air. I looked at the babies; I could almost smell their warm skin from here. I wondered which of them would make it. Those who did would change shape and appearance: taller or shorter; fat or thin; girls or boys. And even though they would each choose their own path, they would always remain somebody's child. They would grow up and grow apart, and would forget, in the same way that they would be forgotten.

Aurelio Ortiz made the sign of the cross and kissed the barrel of his machine gun. In the mountains, sicarios prayed to the Virgin for a straight shot, so he asked for a miracle. Since he couldn't be sure that she would answer his prayer, he grabbed the bat too.

Two German shepherds were barking, tied to a post. He could smell gasoline. The murmurs of a transistor radio and evangelical music could be heard over the cicadas. Maybe everyone had died, and this was a ghost chorus. The cages in the dog pen were empty, their gates thrown open. Tools, drums, and sealed boxes of fertilizer were heaped in the shed.

He peered into the canal but saw only larvae being dragged downstream by the current. A vulture feather covered in dirt fell at his feet; he pushed it away with the toe of his shoe. The feed mill chimneys were puffing out columns of white smoke like crematory ovens. The whole place stank of bird droppings and dried shit, but there was no sign of Abundio's fighting cocks. The Americans and the Malayans had disappeared, the Creoles too. There were just a few feathers floating inside the coop, which had been invaded by wild doves.

At gas stations across the mountains bubbled rumors: Abundio had died, and the irregulars had no leader and were running amok. But nobody said a word about Críspulo, or at least Aurelio hadn't heard anything. Críspulo was the old man's most loyal employee. If he wasn't dead, then where was he hiding?

Aurelio took short steps, trying not to make too much noise, until he tripped in a hole and fell awkwardly on his left foot. Lying on the ground, wincing from the sprain, he heard a snarl. He gripped his 9mm with both hands. Two black Dobermans were loping toward him, baring their drool-covered teeth. From their necks hung broken chains, which dragged behind them on the ground.

Aurelio prayed the way the Mezquite nuns had taught him at school.

"By the sign of the Cross . . ."

He released the safety.

". . . deliver us from our enemies, You who are our God."

The German shepherds tied to the post barked louder.

"In the name of the Father, and of the Son, and of the Holy Spirit . . ."

Grrrrrr. Grrrrrr. Grrrrrrr.

The air was impregnated with the dogs' breath.

Grrrr. Grrrr.

He pressed the trigger.

Grrrr. Grrrr.

The firearm made a hollow, toy-gun sound. The magazine was empty. Turned into easy prey, and frozen in fright, he waited, his only goal to defend himself by swinging the metal bat.

"By the sign of the Cross deliver us from our enemies, You who are our God . . . ," he recited, gripping the bat.

A Kawasaki approached from the highway. When they heard it, the Dobermans ran toward the gate. He seized the moment to run back to the pickup. Once inside, he loaded the gun with a new cartridge. Críspulo got off the bike. With his finger on the trigger, Aurelio wasn't sure whether to shoot over the man's head or blow his brains out.

"By the sign of the Cross deliver us from our enemies, You who are our God . . ."

t was all set. The Cucaña morticians would help me when Consuelo went into labor. In exchange, I was to take care of the body of an eighty-year-old woman that nobody had claimed in three months. It often happened. The morgue received more cadavers than they could freeze, almost all of them elderly abandoned by their families on the border. The families feared deportation if they claimed their dead.

The old lady barely weighed anything, and it didn't take much to move her. Her fingers were missing. They had been removed for fingerprinting. Her abdomen bore a faded vertical scar: through it, the children who had abandoned her on the side of the road had emerged into the world. Her colorless skin showed the protruding bones of a weakened, malnourished being, now stiff and expired, like a promise somebody hadn't kept.

"Who are you? Who left you behind?"

No word of reply escaped her dark mouth. I collected the amputated phalanges and wrapped them in a sheet.

Visitación gave me permission to bring her here. She was the one who prepped the only free grave. She did so whistling and singing her coplas. She was afraid. The irregulars' war was out of control. The irregulars were killing indiscriminately. We were at the mercy of whomever we came across. And not even the Mezquite locals would protect us anymore. If it was true that Abundio had died, then the irregulars would soon come to finish the job the old man had started. When that happened, who would bury us?

Visitación came inside, silent.

"Do you want to see my handiwork?" I asked.

"That's not necessary. You know how to do it right."

After praying an Our Father, we sealed the grave and smoothed the concrete edges. Since we did not know her name or her date of birth, nor the exact date of her death, we inscribed the day, month, and year of her burial into the slab. It was all we had.

"Another without a name," Visitación sighed. "There are more with each passing day."

"If they didn't spare her a thought when she was alive, they won't now that she's dead."

"You're mistaken. Wherever they are, the people who abandoned her will suffer a double blow: what they felt when they left her, and what will grow inside them, once they understand what they've done."

She straightened the mesquite cross on the grave, lit one of her cigars, and sucked in air.

"You didn't want to bury your boys in a cardboard box either. It's not always possible to choose." She exhaled the smoke through her nose. "Gather up everything, Angustias. The morning is well and truly upon us."

We went back to the shed together. The sun was burning hot, and a sooty wind was scouring the cemetery trees. It seemed as if Tolvaneras no longer existed, and I had lost all sense of why I was still here. Time had stopped inside all the clocks.

"I heard talk of your husband yesterday." Visitación was still smoking. "Have you seen anything else strange?" I shook my head. "Keep your eyes open, just in case."

"Do you know something?"

"People talk, that's all. . . ."

"Visitación, look!"

I threw down the shovel and started to run, shouting as I did.

"Angustias, stop! What are you doing?"

A green snake had launched itself from one spiny holdback to another. Consuelo was raking dried leaves directly below.

"Get out of here!" She paid me no mind. "Stop that!"

She looked at me as if I were crazy.

"A snake just sailed over your head! Move it, girl! Do you want to get bitten?"

"There's nothing but clouds here, Angustias. You're losing it." And she kept raking.

"It's not a cloud, you stupid girl! It's a green vine snake!" chimed in Visitación. "They're small and they always look for a warm place to lay their eggs. This girl's always sneaking around in the bushes, surely she knows them."

"I've never seen one before." Consuelo raised her gaze, the rake still between her hands.

Visitación pointed.

"Well, turn around. . . . There's one looking for a nest, and it seems like it found one. There's nothing warmer than a pregnant woman."

The snake uncoiled from the branch. Embedded in its triangular head shone two black eyes like beads against its emerald skin.

Críspulo Miranda threw down his machete. He was pale and his eyes had lost their bilious color. He was a shadow of the man Aurelio had known. He was even skinnier, and his sunken eye sockets looked as if they were devouring his face.

"If you see him where you are, in the afterlife, tell Abundio I tried to save him! Tell him!" he shouted.

The wind loosened several mangoes from the tree, which at that time of year was laden with fruit. Even the wasps seemed agitated. The Indian kneeled, despondent, by his dogs. Aurelio went a few steps closer.

"Críspulo, I'm not dead."

"Don't take me with you!"

"I'm alive, man. I'm not a ghost! Can't you see?"

"That's what ghosts say when they come to drag you away by the leg."

"Where's Abundio?" asked Aurelio.

"At the bottom of the river, with the piranhas. . . ."

"What happened?"

"He was chasing her, and she pushed him into the water. . . ." Críspulo's story was confusing, feverish.

"Who is 'she'? What are you talking about?"

"I'll tell you anything you want to know, just don't take me with you."

The night the irregulars took Mezquite, Mono turned up with his men at Abundio's farm to demand the land at Tolvaneras.

"They had pistols, but so did we." Now Críspulo smiled. "Don Abundio took out the rifle, but he missed, and Mono responded with a blast to his arm. Our men pulled out their guns, and the shoot-out started. The dogs hadn't eaten for three days. They were hungry. . . ." Críspulo kissed the Doberman. "Roco and Azufre didn't even leave Mono's men with lips to laugh with. Only one of them escaped alive. Even better . . . that way he would tell everyone what had happened."

"Who else was there that night?"

"Doña Mercedes and the girl. . . ."

On hearing the shots, Abundio's wife ran to his office. When she went inside, one of the dogs was tearing into what was left of Mono's face. She started screaming and her shrieks triggered her husband's fury.

Aurelio knew enough about Alcides Abundio to imagine what had happened. Missing his shot at Mono would have enraged him, but Mercedes's cries would only have made things worse.

"'I'm going to kill you!'" Críspulo made as if he were wielding a gun. "Don Abundio repeated it several times. And I followed them."

Mercedes ran to the riverbank, headed for the neighbor's land. The waters roiled. It was not a good idea to go in at that time of year. Abundio was wounded and stumbling, and even so he pursued her, his gun in hand. Mercedes managed to put some distance between them, but then she slipped in the mud and her husband caught up, grabbing hold of her. The exertion, together with his hemorrhaging arm, which only bled more profusely, had sapped his strength. He enveloped her like a wet cloth.

"Abundio tried to hit her, but she grabbed him by his wounded arm and sank her nails in. They fought like cat and dog and fell into the water together."

Críspulo fell silent. He was a rag doll once more.

"Piranhas smell blood, and Abundio had lost a lot. . . . They were eaten in seconds. They screamed until they sank beneath the water."

"You didn't help them?"

Críspulo stroked the dogs' backs.

"Did you help them or not?"

"That's why you've come looking for me, you're here to take me to hell. That's it, isn't it?" He removed a flask of anisette from his pocket and took a swig. "I didn't help him." He drank some more. "Perpetua was the one who called the ambulance."

The alcohol lit up his eyes.

"Mercedes died just as her mother did. They're together now, at the bottom of the river . . . ," he whimpered. "And the old man is dead."

"And the girl? Where is she?"

"Don't take her too, not her!"

"Where is she, Críspulo?"

The Indian rubbed his forehead with his hands. He was soaked in sweat and gave off the same stink as his dogs.

"Get out of here, ghost! Leave!"

"Críspulo . . . I'm alive! Can't you see?"

"Get back!" He waved his arms to frighten him away.

Like his beasts, cruelty no longer affected Críspulo. He pulled on the dogs' chains and tied them to the tree along with the German shepherds, turned around, and looked at Aurelio.

"If you're dead, then why do you ask what you already know?"

"Show me the girl. . . ." Aurelio took out his gun and aimed it at him. "Take me to Carmen."

Críspulo had finally become prey. He raised his arms and sat down with his dogs.

"Where is Carmen?" repeated Aurelio.

"I'm not going anywhere with Beelzebub."

He released the safety but paused. Críspulo was practically dead already. Hunger, guilt, or his own animals would finish him off. The most feared farmhand in the mountains had become a ghost who longed to die.

The pistol still in hand, Aurelio checked what was left of the cages and skirted the canal of dirty water. He found nothing. If the girl was still alive, she had to be somewhere in the kennel. He searched among the bags and in the storage shed. He didn't find her there either.

At the far end of the field, he saw a small farmhouse made of concrete blocks. He kicked open the door. The place smelled like dogs. There wasn't even a window for ventilation, and the only furniture was a table and a mattress. On the earthen floor, Aurelio caught sight of something out of place. He crouched to see it better: it was a flute carved from wood.

The fish that were still alive flapped back and forth inside the baskets. The women mended the nets as quickly as they could, deft with their threads and knives. Visitación addressed one of them.

"María Angula, what's going on? What's all this?"

"The fish are back!"

Catfish, bass, and rays were lashing the river water with their tails, and the white water near the shore teemed with sardines. I got out of the pickup with a shovel, to collect some fish too. Everyone in town had turned out. We bumped into one another, our skin glistening beneath the sun as if we had scales too.

To land more of them, Visitación and I drove closer to shore, where fishermen were swarming with nets and small boats. After years of drought, the river had finally come back to life. It was hot, and the sky was pressing down on us with its water vapor and sand.

Consuelo brought us a glass of papeleón with a squeeze of lemon that Visitación gulped down, not bothering to say thank you.

"Angustias, you have a drink too!"

The wedges of lemon and pieces of panela dissolved in my mouth like a gift. I wanted to finish it but left the last sip for Consuelo. There were still a lot of fish to collect, a desperate miracle that nearly overwhelmed us. Whether or not heaven and the saints were behind it scarcely mattered. These fish worked the same effect as the Palo de Mayo rains: they eased tensions and blended one truth with another. The irregulars would come to kill us, but not today.

I headed for Mezquite's main square, the pickup now full. I could smell soil and guts.

In the fish market, fishermen were removing the scales, which sprang from the fish like sequins turned iridescent in the midday light. Then they stripped out the guts with shears and cut off the heads with a heavy thud.

When I unloaded the last box of bass, I heard strains of music, isolated sounds that didn't turn into a song. I glanced down the walkways, but nobody was there.

Before we departed, in one of the side mirrors, I saw Jairo tuning his accordion. He was missing his right arm, and a bloody bandage covered his eyes. I wanted to get out, but I could not. The door handles were burning, and fire was licking the hood. I tried to force open the doors and break the glass. But I could not. Jairo did nothing to help me.

"Angustias, wake up. There are no fish here." Consuelo shook me awake. A nightmare, again.

Outside, the wind was rocking the treetops.

He rang the doorbell three times. Gladys was wearing a patterned dressing gown and looked under the weather. She locked eyes with him for a few seconds, then shut the door in his face and locked it. Aurelio persevered, but she threatened to call the police chief. The new mayor, she shouted at him, had been instructed to throw him in prison for treachery and corruption.

"Open up! I need to talk to you!"

"Out of here, you crook!"

Gladys spoke as if she were innocent. Neither party was, and they both knew it. But fear had wiped his receptionist's mind clean, for suddenly she had forgotten all the false invoices she had written at Abundio's behest.

Now that Abundio was dead, the irregulars were increasingly active. They hired themselves out to the highest bidder, stoking fear wherever they went. Allied with the smugglers, they made demands on the new mayor, Liberio Mójica: they wouldn't touch the town so long as the border and Tolvaneras were left to them. If that was the price for peace, Mójica was prepared to pay it.

Aurelio's replacement was a provincial politician. Abundio had scorned him for being a bootlicker. He started out heading parks and recreation and from there moved up the ranks to councillor of social planning and community development. He lined his pockets at the expense of outpatient clinics, collecting enough to buy a house and three establishments on the town's main street.

He had never aspired to be mayor—Mójica preferred low-profile roles, which made stealing easier—but once in office, he summed up Abundio's death with a formula the press transcribed word for word: "A tragic incident, a product of the commotion and chaos into which Aurelio Ortiz's administration plunged this town and its inhabitants." A twisted version of events that exonerated Abundio from the racketeering that he too had profited from.

He said not a word about the hacienda assault, much less about the armed attack on the town; nor did he mention the waves of walkers flooding the region or the smugglers who trafficked in those people's luck. He promptly had the three black crosses scrubbed from the city hall facade; had a court order issued against Aurelio Ortiz; and arranged for the immediate construction of a statue in honor of Alcides Abundio, benefactor and great man of Mezquite.

Both the Fabres hacienda and the old textile mills would be overseen by the local government from that point forward, until justice was served. The investigations into Reyes, the priest, and Víctor Hugo's deaths were buried in endless red tape. Críspulo Miranda was presumed out of his mind, and the custody of Carmen, Alcides Abundio's only legitimate heir, was given to her mother's sisters. Neither of them collected her in person, instead they sent a lawyer.

All was at peace, a peace that also reigned in the graves.

e found Jairo at the ferias del arroz, local dances that were celebrated on the district outskirts, attended by men and women wanting to blow their money on aguardiente and bazuco. He had to buy him several rounds in a bar packed with cockfighting aficionados before Jairo would tell him anything about Angustias and Visitación.

"I know as much as you do."

Aurelio Ortiz was a coward, but he wasn't stupid. Whether out of fear or greed, Jairo was lying.

"I haven't seen them for days. . . . And in all the confusion, people have barely said a word about them." The coplero knocked back his drink.

"The city council I was once mayor of has an arrest warrant out for me, and the irregulars have a target on my head. I don't have time for bullshit."

"I know they're alive."

Aurelio held out a bill.

"Why are you so interested?" Jairo glanced at the money. "You didn't let Angustias bury her sons in peace, and you threw Visitación out of her cemetery. Why the change of heart?"

Aurelio stood. He had heard enough sermons.

"The bottle is paid for; it's all yours."

The coplero took him by the shoulder and lowered his voice.

"The last time I saw them was the night the irregulars took Mezquite."

The cockfight was about to start. Aurelio motioned for Jairo to continue.

"I went with them to bury the man they took to your office. On the way back, I told Angustias what everyone was saying: that her husband has taken up with the irregulars. . . ."

"Have you seen him?"

"No, but people talk." He lowered his voice again: "He was the only one who made it out alive from the assault on Abundio's hacienda. That's what people are saying—that he was there."

"How could they know? Nobody knows him."

"They say it's the same man who showed up in town with Angustias. Plus, he has an eastern accent."

"What did Angustias say when you told her?"

"She was furious, but then the accident happened."

"What accident?"

"Didn't you know? We were run off the road on our way to Nopales."

Aurelio filled his glass but could not bring it to his lips. The headlights shone in his mind. So they were the ones he saw on the side of the road that night, the ones he did nothing to help.

"Are you listening to me?"

"You said you were run off the road. . . ."

"Since then, I haven't heard anything from Visitación or Angustias."

"Have you been back to Mezquite?"

"What, to get myself killed? Everyone's messed up in that town."

Aurelio wanted to cover his back, so he filled the coplero's pockets.

"Listen, Jairo. . . ." He moved closer. "Say I'm dead. Make up whatever you want: a copla, some other song, whatever you feel like, but make sure you include that I'm a soul in torment."

"What for?"

"None of your business. Sing that you've seen me drinking alone at the bar, that I appear in two places at once. All that bullshit that people like to believe."

He slipped another bill into the accordion bellows and exited through the back. In the arena, bloody and almost blind, the two fighting cocks kept pecking each other.

onsuelo's belly was growing at odds with the rest of her body. While the baby increased in mass, she only shrank. Her belly looked like a huge blister. To get under her skin, Visitación started calling her Little Virgin.

"That little baby has been planted by the Holy Spirit . . . hasn't it, sweetie?"

Not even that worked: Visitación was itching to know where the girl had come from, or who might come calling when the hour arrived, yet Consuelo gave nothing away.

"Not long now until the birth, and you haven't even decided on a name!"

"When she is born, she will have one," responded Consuelo, playing dumb. "Maybe I should call her Pentecostés to make you happy, doña, since you love the Bible so much."

We had broken no bones in the accident, but it had left the possibility of a family between us shattered beyond repair.

"You brought her here, so you'll take her away too," grumbled Visitación, pointing at me.

"What do you want? Why so much fighting?"

"For her to go."

"If she had arrived here wrapped in a shroud, you would have accepted her then, wouldn't you?"

"Wake up, Angustias. She'll no sooner give birth than sell or do who knows what to the baby."

Women fleeing the plague were raped on the byways and illegal routes. It was the toll for moving from the world they were fleeing into the one they sought. Abortions were illegal. Most of the women who tried ended up bleeding out in clandestine clinics. Those who gave birth left their uteruses behind in the emergency ward, and those who were marginally luckier were taken away and forced to sell their babies.

Children were cost-effective. It didn't take much to raise them, and they were quick to learn. They provided cruel, cheap labor for crime. The smugglers and irregulars created their own black market with them: they brought them better returns than the walkers. That was why it was impossible to rid Visitación of the notion that Consuelo had an arrangement in place and was using us as a cover.

"You're not going to say anything?"

I crossed my arms and was quiet, for the good of the three of us.

"You have until tomorrow to tell her to leave. And if you don't, I will."

She grabbed her shovel and got up without another word.

The boys' grave had never looked better. That morning Consuelo did away with the grime, using a wet rag to scrub their names and rubbing at their dates of birth and death until they gleamed.

"What are you doing?"

"Cleaning."

Not turning around to look at me, she rinsed the rag, squeezed it, and kept scrubbing the cement.

"Do you want me to leave too?" Dribbles of water made furrows in the sand.

"What makes you say that?"

I sat down next to her. She turned her head and looked at me with her large, dark eyes.

"I heard you and Visitación talking. . . ."

"In that case, you know I said nothing of the sort."

"I am *not* going to sell the baby like Visitación says. I don't know what I'll do when she's born, but I'm certainly not going to dump her in the trash."

"You should leave. You can't give birth in a cemetery, and this is no place to raise a child. I'll help you. There's not much time. You'll go into labor any day now."

She nodded.

"When I finish here, I'll gather my things."

"Be quick about it," I said. "We'll leave in an hour."

I walked among the graves at Tolvaneras. There were so many more than when I first arrived. I knew every one of the names and dates scratched into the slabs; their stories too, and the circumstances surrounding their arrival. But when I thought of the dead in The Third Country, I didn't feel any of the things Visitación spoke of. I didn't want justice or mercy for them.

There was one and only one truth, and nothing could change it: all these men and women were dead, and they were never coming back. That was the only sure thing, and there was nothing Visitación or anyone could do to change it. The dead were not hers. They did not belong to those who cursed them or longed for them. Not even my sons were entirely mine, even if they were the reason I had remained here.

Life was not the way Visitación described: it was fleeting, something that could be snuffed out. This was why her words and speeches didn't ring true to me. I was only interested in keeping alive my memories of the babies I loved. They hadn't lived long enough for me to tell them I loved them. For as long as I stayed close to the foot of their grave, they would live on in my head. That was enough for me. I was indifferent to everything else, or at least so I had believed, until I met Consuelo.

told Visitación I would be back in a couple of hours and waited for Consuelo by the spiny holdbacks. She got into the pickup without asking where we were headed, resigned to a fate I had yet to explain to her.

At that time of day, the road toward Cucaña was clear. Not even the scrap dealers were around. I changed gears and checked the mirrors. Nobody was following us.

"Are you okay?"

Consuelo was clutching a backpack and looking out the window, her unfocused gaze on the fences outside.

"I've found a place where you can stay until you go into labor. It's a shelter for pregnant women."

"One of the army ones?"

"Yes, one of those."

"Do you want me to get deported? Or, even worse, for them to send me back to the children's shelter?"

"If you don't turn up, or if you escape, both of us will be deported. I've registered you as my daughter." Consuelo took out a bottle of water and took a sip. "I'll take you there. I won't be able to stay with you because I have to return the pickup. Visitación can't be on her own, isolated at the cemetery."

"You're going to dump me there. That's what all this is about, isn't it?"

"I'll come back tonight! You have to promise me you won't leave."

"And how will you come back, if you won't have the pickup?"

"I'll find a way. The important thing is that we get you to Cucaña as soon as possible, and that once there, you stay put."

She listened to me, not saying anything for a while. Then she motioned at the dash.

"It's a long way to Cucaña. We only have half a tank, and the drums are empty. Aren't you going to fill them?"

I flipped on the turn signal and pulled into the only gas station in the area.

Arapping on the window woke him. Aurelio sat up, alert, his pistol in hand. It was a young man offering to clean his windshield, that was all. He checked the time on his watch: ten fifteen in the morning. A line of men and women were waiting to fill their drums with fuel. There were still three trucks in line before him. The wait seemed interminable.

He leaned his head back on the glass and tried to sleep, but it was impossible. He passed the time watching people trying to get gas. They were carrying up to two or three containers in each hand. Since the irregulars started hijacking fuel trucks to extort the gas station owners, prices had skyrocketed, and the resale value on the black market provided another way to make a living.

Some people had slept at the gas station to keep their position in the line. Those who had only just arrived would spend the entire morning beneath the hot sun that roasted the asphalt. There was no guarantee they would leave with anything, no guarantee that there was fuel enough to last until their turn, but there they were, staked to the spot.

The gas station had only one employee. The more he refueled the pickups and rust buckets, the longer the line of men, women, and children grew, all intent on reselling whatever fuel they procured. Ten gallons provided enough to live on for at least a week. Everyone smelled like gasoline, and a single match would have been enough to send them all up in flames, but nobody moved from their spot.

A gray pickup drove by the fuel pumps. Aurelio looked in the rearview: it was Angustias Romero. He hid his pistol beneath his shirt and pulled a dark cap down low over his eyes. His mouth felt pasty, and before he stepped out, he rubbed a little toothpaste on his teeth. He climbed out, walked over to the gray pickup, peered in with caution, and tapped the window with his knuckles. The pieces of the man he had become suddenly came together when Angustias looked him head to toe.

"We have to talk."

"Go on," she answered, her hands glued to the wheel.

"Not here. I'll wait for you around the back, at the air pumps."

They met three hours later in the parking lot. They spoke out their windows. Visitación was fine, and nothing major had gone down at the cemetery, Angustias said, getting it off her chest. Tolvaneras still didn't have an owner, Aurelio told her. Angustias was in a hurry.

"I can't talk now. I need to get to Cucaña."

"At this rate you'll run out of gas."

"I've got enough," she answered bluntly.

"Why the hurry?"

"Consuelo's due any day now, I have to get her there as soon as possible. I'll be back in a couple of hours, to find some clothes and things. You know, women's things."

Aurelio glanced at the pregnant girl, silent in the passenger seat. She didn't seem as intimidating as she had the other day, when she was shouting, a shovel in hand, defending Visitación and Angustias on the steps of city hall.

The women who had brought about his ruin were still alive, and so was he. It was time to make peace.

"I'll drive you back to Cucaña, Angustias. When you're on your way back to Tolvaneras, stop here. I'll be waiting."

She nodded, turned the key in the ignition, and drove away. Aurelio watched as she headed at full speed for the border.

Consuelo's water broke after we left the gas station. Lying back in the passenger seat, she inhaled through her nose and exhaled through her mouth, as if she were trying to scare off the pain with her breaths. The closer together her exhalations, the harder I pressed my foot on the accelerator. The distance between us and the border would be measured in contractions, not miles.

The Cucaña maternity ward was a four-story concrete building, a gray, dreary place. The walls were covered in broken tiles, and rusty gurneys were staggered along the corridors beside trash cans. The morticians had kept their word and booked a place in the birthing suite, just as we had agreed. The nurse I spoke to about the arrangement jotted down Consuelo's name and date of birth. Then he took us through the back.

When the time came, she would give birth in the hospital. Until then, they would leave her in a tent erected by the army for displaced persons from the eastern mountains, among those who already had a number and were waiting, crowded inside. The place was packed, there was barely any space between the beds. The women's moans joined as one, as if they were praying a novena in wails.

I lay Consuelo on the bed, holding her by the waist. Her dress, tight against her swollen body, crept up her thighs, revealing her swollen legs. She took a sip of water and tucked the plastic bottle into her backpack.

"I'll be back in three hours. Don't do anything stupid."

She waved goodbye, the weight of her body sinking her into the bare mattress.

On the door, a handwritten list detailed the tasks that had to be carried out and what items the patients should bring with them: towels, soap, bandages, trash bags. Outside, lying on the waiting room benches, surrounded by clouds of flies, two women dozed under dust-covered blankets. Another, her lips painted pink, cried out in pain, pressing her hands, with their dirty fingernails, into her belly. She called for help before collapsing.

Most of the women were here alone, though some were accompanied by their mothers, who were reciting the half dozen hospitals that had turned them away. Their daughters couldn't give birth in the street, they cried. The nurses, their uniforms bloodstained, asked for a patience they no longer had. Instead of a maternity ward, it seemed like a place people went to die.

urelio was waiting where we had agreed, and he followed me to Tolvaneras. I couldn't understand why he wanted to talk to me, or why on earth he was offering me help. But I didn't ask questions. He had more to lose than we did, and I had nobody else to take me back to the border once I had returned the pickup.

I was the first to leave the gas station. He joined me a few minutes later. On the way to the cemetery, we crossed paths with no one. It was still daytime, but there was no trace of other pickup trucks or buses, only the carts pulled by donkeys and horses that herders and tinsmiths use to shift junk from one place to another.

When we arrived at the gates to The Third Country, Aurelio parked his pickup and waited, the engine running. I drove through to the spiny holdback, unloaded the drums of gasoline, and hid them beneath some tarpaulins. Then I locked the driver's door and walked over to the shed. Visitación was smoking, seated on the curb, her arms resting on her knees.

"Who's this?" She motioned with her lips.

"Aurelio Ortiz."

Visitación sized me up and dragged hard on her cigarette until a red circle flared. A column of ash fell to the ground.

"I'll be back in two days, once Consuelo has given birth."

"I knew it," she snorted. "Angustias Romero and her secret dealings, you sure do like to get tied up in other people's problems!"

"The pickup has a half tank of gas, in case you need it. There's more in the drums."

She let out a few laughs as she adjusted her colorful headscarf. I moved closer to say goodbye.

"Out of here, you smell like gasoline and I'm smoking!" she shouted, waving her arms about.

I placed the keys on the hood and walked over to Aurelio. If we left within the hour, we would reach Cucaña before midnight.

"Angustias!"

I turned around.

Visitación looked at me, her cigarette still in hand.

"Vaya con dios!"

"He always rides with somebody else, doña."

Angustias Romero collapsed into the passenger seat. She fell asleep with her hands on her lap, her head tilted back. She had driven the road that connected Mezquite to Cucaña, then had turned around and driven it again in reverse. Her skin was burned, her gum boots too big, and her clothing smelled like fuel.

When Aurelio Ortiz met her, she was full of the life that had just been snatched from her. Something in that dried-up woman had numbed until it had scarred over.

They hit a pothole as big as a crater, jolting her awake.

"Where are we?" She rubbed her eyes, still sleepy.

"There's still an hour to go, keep sleeping."

Angustias fiddled with the radio but couldn't get it to work. Outside, the mountains had changed with the setting of the sun. Darkness had smoothed over the dun-colored mountain peaks and the gashes of the rock faces.

"Stop the car," she ordered. "I need to go . . . you know."

Aurelio urinated on one side of the pickup, she on the other. They got back in without exchanging a word. The mats were covered in crumbs and candy wrappers. By the gearshift, Angustias saw the empty packet of a toothbrush, and a box of antacid was lurching on the dash.

"People are saying you're a soul in torment. . . ."

"That's thanks to Jairo. He did me a favor."

"He doesn't do favors."

"You're right. . . . Let's say it was a commission. That's more precise." Aurelio stepped on the gas. "Things are not so great between you two, are they?"

Angustias snorted and looked at the hills.

"Why did you come back?"

"To tie up a few loose ends."

"Do you want your job back? Are you looking for money?"

"Neither. I came for Tolvaneras."

"Are you going to try to force us out of there again?"

He shook his head.

"My father died convinced that I was a coward. He wasn't wrong. I didn't do right by you or Visitación. My first mistake, Angustias, was closing the cemetery. My second, opening it again."

He glanced in the rearview and side mirrors. He was doing so at regular intervals.

"Before, Visitación had two enemies: Abundio and the irregulars. When the old man died, the irregulars became even more dangerous."

Angustias grabbed the empty toothbrush packet and tossed it out the window.

"If you don't want to close down Tolvaneras, then why are you here?"

"It would have been easy to reach an agreement with Mójica, but he does whatever the smugglers and irregulars say."

"Like you when you were mayor. I don't see any difference."

Aurelio took that one on the chin.

"Before, each side had a leader: Mono and Abundio. Not anymore. How can we find out what they want when we don't know who's in charge?"

"Why do you care? Why don't you just leave with your wife and children? You didn't help us when you should have, so why do so now?"

"If for once I'm righting wrongs, at least have a little faith that my intentions are good."

"What you've got isn't good intentions. It's guilt." Aurelio tried to interrupt her, but she wouldn't let him. "Why are you telling me all this and not Visitación? Why are you helping me, and what do you want in return?"

What Aurelio desired could not be traded for. His sleepless nights did not equal two drums of gasoline or four rusty shovels. And what he wanted—for his sons to look at him with respect, for his wife not to scrutinize him like a thief, for ghosts not to pile up in his rearview mirrors—could not be counted or hoarded. He wanted to be respectable, that was all.

When he had the chance, he didn't help her bury her boys. He showed up with an entourage to frighten her off. Nor did he do anything when she and Visitación ran off the road in the middle of the night. Now that it was within his power to alleviate someone's suffering, he was not about to stand back with arms crossed.

"People talk about your husband. . . ."

She squirmed in her seat.

"Let me finish."

"What would you know?"

"People think your husband is a guerrilla. Have you seen him?" Angustias didn't answer. "He left without saying anything?"

"He never did say much."

"Did you have a disagreement?"

"It's impossible to have a disagreement with a sick man. The only thing you can do is put up with him. And that was what I did the whole way here: carry deadweight. Three deadweights! But at least my sons were too young to be able to help it."

"Do you know if he's been back to the cemetery? In Sangre de Cristo they're saying he's been seen wandering around with no work or food. That he sleeps in the street and carves figurines with a knife."

"Salveiro doesn't even know how to cut up an orange," lied Angustias.

"I heard that, in a cockfight Abundio organized, your husband went berserk and slit the throats of three men. He did it cruelly, shouting threats."

"It's not possible," she said several times. "Salveiro has no will, how could he be capable of killing someone?"

"Whenever he slashed at the drunks he came across, he said he was 'Talkalot.' That's the same name the irregulars call one of their own: a man who butchers people without a word. . . . The day you buried your boys, Visitación called him 'Talkalot' in front of everyone, didn't she?"

Angustias's face was rigid and pale. Her lips were moving, but nothing came out.

"I don't know if your husband has been back to the cemetery. If he has, maybe he has unfinished business, or the irregulars sent him. But I do know that the children he had with you are buried at Tolvaneras. That could be it."

"If I asked you right now where your two boys and your wife are, would you tell me?" Now Aurelio was the one to fall silent. "See? Now, imagine I'd shown up at your sons' burial with three dogs. Would you trust me then? Well, there you go. Take me to Cucaña, and we'll call the whole thing even."

Angustias Romero took a whiff of her shirt to see if that was where the smell was coming from. She stank of gasoline. Just one spark, and everything would light up.

The clock struck three in the morning at the Cucaña hospital. With no news, they waited the way the hopeless do.

"You've said what you had to say. Now go. You have no unfinished business with me."

Aurelio didn't have the strength to answer. Several years of exhaustion had made his body go limp. He stayed where he was because he could no longer leave, because it was early morning, because somebody might shoot him, because he did not want to abandon this woman. She did not need him, he knew that. But it didn't matter.

He tried to sleep in vain, but instead he watched Angustias Romero, who paced the corridor with her eyes fixed on her boots. She was focused on that single task of coming and going. "They said I would be allowed to go through. Why haven't they called?" he heard her murmur.

It was five a.m., and nobody else had appeared in the corridor. Angustias disappeared, hunting for news. Rigid in his plastic chair, Aurelio felt useless. The moans and cries of women in labor seemed better suited to a war hospital than a maternity ward. He wondered if his boys were missing him, if his eldest had kept catching guacucos on the shore, and if the Wayuu women were crisscrossing the highway at this hour to peddle their colorful baskets. He thought about his Mezquite house, now sacked by the irregulars. Everything he had to his name would have disappeared.

What do fathers do in maternity wards? Do they cry out too? He wouldn't know. He couldn't remember how long it had taken his wife to give birth to their boys. Not the eldest, not the littlest. He was there both times, but he was incapable of saying whether his wife had cried out, or if at any stage she had been afraid or in pain. Salvación had never told him, and he had never expressed any interest in finding out.

The last time they spoke, she had not even asked him when he would be back.

S alveiro didn't make it in time. I wasn't due for a few weeks, and neither of us thought they would come early. As I rinsed a woman's hair, I felt little nips inside my belly, like the boys were struggling to exit my body. When I finished with my customers, I closed the salon and hailed a taxi.

I don't know how I reached the operating room; I only remember that once I was there, the nurses scraped a disposable blade across my crotch. Rather than shave me, they seemed determined to skin me completely. Lying on the bed, I kept my eyes on the fluorescence emanating from the lights in the ceiling, neon tubes covered in dust. I didn't know who would look after me. Nor was I aware of the time. I was thirsty and experiencing intense pain, as if nails were being driven between my pubis and back. The doctor called me by name, but I didn't know his and could see only his eyes, which peered at me from above his mask.

My body wouldn't obey. Sometimes it shook on its own, other times a nurse told me when to push. I felt as if the birth were taking years. Machines emitted beeps at irregular intervals.

"Call the anesthetist," said the doctor.

The nurse left, and when she returned it was alongside a man who proceeded to have her fix a tube to my arm, into which he emptied the contents of a syringe. The machine kept beeping, faster and faster.

"Tell the cardiologist to come down."

"What's going on?" I asked the nurse. "Have you told my husband?"

"He's outside," she lied.

"Not long now, Angustias. Breathe."

The doctor sank the scalpel in, but I felt nothing. Time ticked by, I didn't know how much. A minute? An hour? Two? Higinio came out first, not crying. The doctor rushed him to a crib and pressed his chest several times. With Salustio, that wasn't necessary. His heart was beating, at least.

Standing before a clock as it struck six in the morning, I thought about my sons. I couldn't get them out of my head. It seemed like a bad sign. Knowing that Consuelo was giving birth made them reappear in my mind as if I had never buried them. They had now been gone for more time than I had held them in my arms. So much pain for such a short life. Anyone would say I brought them into the world just so I could lay my eyes on them.

I walked back down the white-tiled corridor. Aurelio was asleep in the chair. He was wearing a ridiculous hat that only served to raise suspicion. I felt sorry for him. I had no right to judge.

From the end of the corridor came the screams. There seemed to echo hundreds of them, effort repeated by birthing women for all those who had given birth before them. I thought about my mother and wondered whether a deaf woman cries out when she brings a child into this world.

Drops collected from the ceiling into soda bottles that were acting as makeshift buckets. The persistent sound of the drops hitting the surface marked the passing of a time knocked out of step. Consuelo was babbling and waving her arms. I moved closer to her and spoke in a soft voice very slowly, like the doctors had instructed. She was sedated, but she could hear. They would keep her like this until they had ascertained the damage.

The little girl was born breathing, but it was not clear whether Consuelo would live. The birth was long and complicated, they explained.

Seated next to her bed, I let her know I had seen her daughter in the neonatal nursery, that she had been wrapped in a blanket that had fish on it, and that she was the most beautiful of them all.

"You have to wake up, so you can see her. We should call her Milagros, don't you think?"

Expecting a response was absurd. She was trapped in a sticky membrane of exhaustion and sedatives. She tried to wrench the tubes that attached her to the machines. I grabbed her hands and patted them until she grew calm. She was gaunt, disheveled, and pale. Barely covered by a paper gown, her nude figure seemed to have suddenly aged years. I passed my hand over her forehead several times. Like I had once done with my boys, I sang:

White dove
With the little blue crest
Take me on your wings
To see Jesus.

Consuelo, so small, though not so small that she would fit into a shoebox. Her own mother gone from one day to the next, and she forcibly made one.

The nurse came in to tell me I should leave the room. I kissed Consuelo's burning forehead and went out to the corridor, thinking of the bird whistle. I would have liked to blow it for her.

A ngustias sat down next to Aurelio Ortiz. In one hand she had the death certificate and in the other, a plastic bag containing a rucksack and a cotton dress. She folded the piece of paper, tucked it into her back pocket, and opened the rucksack. Inside was a bottle of water, a tissue, and an empty coin purse.

"Will you take me back to Tolvaneras?"

Aurelio nodded and stood.

"I'll come back for Consuelo tomorrow. Right now, I have no way to take her with me."

It was almost noon when they left the maternity ward, she with the baby girl in her arms, he wearing his cap and dark glasses.

By the pickup, leaning on the bed, Jairo was waiting for them. He was carrying the accordion and had a brazen smile on his face. His smile disappeared when he saw the baby.

The three blinked at one another.

"I thought I recognized your pickup, and figured I'd wait for you."

"What do you want?"

"Money. A ghost's upkeep doesn't come cheap." He looked at Angustias. "Is he yours?"

"He's a she, Consuelo's daughter."

"And why isn't she here?"

"Because she's dead."

Aurelio Ortiz took Jairo by the arm and shoved him behind the pickup.

"You want money? Here's your damned money!" He dug his

hand into his pocket and threw a few bills in his face. "Now, get out of here."

Jairo gathered up the money and counted.

"Remember," warned Aurelio, "I'm a spook . . . and Angustias Romero is too."

"I never saw you. Either of you."

He scurried away, like one of the rats that ran around the market.

In Cucaña, everything was the same: the uncouth stallholders, the hairdressers who paid for hair by the weight, the women who got into the trailers and ran to the ladies' room afterward, the walkers driven by the plague to this side of the mountains: they were ghosts too.

The sun heated the asphalt until a mirage appeared, the same one that made fish and snakes fly over the rivers and trees at Tolvaneras. Seated beside Aurelio, Angustias was rocking the baby.

He glanced at her out of the corner of his eye. She didn't notice. She was too busy feeding the little girl with the milk they had given her at the hospital. The bottle clashed with her work boots and calloused knuckles. Outside, in the world that existed beyond the window, withered sandpaper trees that would be reduced to coals flitted past, but the woman and child gave off a peace that even he was capable of perceiving.

Angustias Romero turned to him.

"Aurelio, look at all her hair!"

For the first time, he saw her smile.

Black smoke billowed into the sky above Tolvaneras. The shed was in flames, as were the spiny holdbacks, and a scorched smell of gas impregnated everything. I wound up the windows.

"Go back a ways, Aurelio. Don't let the girl breathe in this filth."

"Stay here with her. I'll go in."

"You're no longer mayor, and in this place, I'm the boss."

He took a 9mm pistol out of the glove box, slid back the slide, and passed it to me.

"You only need to pull the trigger. You have nine shots."

"If by nightfall I haven't returned, leave. Don't entertain the thought of going in. Take her as far away as possible."

He nodded and took the baby into his arms. I hid the weapon beneath my shirt and ran toward the cemetery.

The Third Country was being consumed by flames, which were being whipped up by the wind. Visitación's pickup had been transformed into a lump of smoking metal, and the drums of gasoline, into a blackish paste. There was no trace of tires on the sand; no casings either. Only soot.

The fire had reached the shed, but the lean-to where we slept was still standing.

I went in with the hope of finding Visitación lying on the sleeping mat, but she wasn't there. After a long search, I found her about three hundred feet from the shed. Her eyes were frozen open. She was still wearing her colorful headscarf, and the wasps were crawling over her cheeks.

I walked around in the smoke with the pistol at my back, tucked into the waistband of my pants. I ran to my sons' grave. Before Higinio and Salustio's burial chamber, Salveiro was waiting, seated on the sand. He was missing a few teeth, and his eyes were dead too.

"Angustias, it's me, Talkalot."

He had a knife in his hand and his face was smeared with soot. He wasn't wearing a uniform or a pistol, only a disguise of grimy military gear branded with the regular army emblem, patched clothing, and dirty boots.

"Do you like the figurines? They're lovely, don't you think?" He showed me two snakes carved from wood.

"Yes, Salveiro. They're lovely."

The flames crackled like crumpled paper. Salveiro got to his feet and looked at me, the knife still in his hand.

"What did you do with the boxes?" he asked.

"They're safe."

"Where?"

"Around here. . . ."

"Can you show me? I want to see them." He picked up a stone.

"I'll show you, but before I do, answer me this: When you arrived here, was the fire already burning?"

He shook his head from one side to the other as he filed the blade against the rock.

"Did you light the fire?"

"I don't remember. Are you going to show me the boxes or not?"

"First, I need to know one more thing." I breathed heavily. "Was Visitación . . ."

"Alive? Yes."

I moved my hand to my back and grasped the pistol.

"Did you come here alone?"

"I know the way. I don't need anyone to show it to me. Where are the boxes? *I want to see the boxes!*" He threw the stone. "Show me the boys. Where did you hide them? They're my sons too!"

"They're dead. We buried them together. Don't you remember?"

"I said show me the boxes!"

He raised the knife.

"The old lady took them from us, but I'm going to take them back. Them, and you. Bring me the boxes, Angustias! We're going home!" He moved toward me, the knife still in hand.

I pulled out the gun and fired. One, two, three, four, five times. A red borehole appeared in the space above his eyebrows, quickly flooding them.

My legs were shaking and sweat clouded my vision. I went to the shed, grabbed a burning branch, and held it to his clothing. The guerrilla getup caught fire instantly.

Finally, we could rest in peace—all four of us.

Visitación Salazar still looked as if she were made from oil and jet. Her skin shone beneath the diesel sun that lay waste to Tolvaneras. She had several wounds in her chest, the deepest of which still bled. She had buried my children and taught me to bury those of others; now I owed her the same courtesy.

The shed had been reduced to a charcoal skeleton. The tools—no more than twisted metal—were now useless for digging a ditch.

I removed her colorful headscarf and used it to rub the sticky mess of blood and dust from her face. Just as she had shown me, I brought her arms and legs together to make her appear as if she were sleeping.

There was still one last chamber hidden in the baby columbarium. I had made it myself, very close to my boys, so that I could be buried there when the time came. I scraped at the dirt with a broken shovel and mixed it with the previous day's cement. It was hot, and the wind was still fueling the fire. I churned the wet mix until I had something resembling mortar.

I covered her face with her colorful scarf, shrouded her with the only blanket in the shed that had not burned, and placed her in the grave. I smoothed the gravestone with a small trail, whistling the songs she liked, and with a spiny holdback stick, wrote: VISITACIÓN SALAZAR (1959–2019).

I turned around and started walking toward the road.

On the far side, Aurelio Ortiz sat waiting for me in his pickup, the baby girl cradled in his arms.

A Note from the Translator

Karina Sainz Borgo's *No Place to Bury the Dead* is both a return to form and a departure from her first novel. Once more, she paints her narrative world in bold strokes, but this time the subject matter, if not the canvas, is larger. There are more characters, more locations, and more entanglements. Her interest is again focused on a crumbling world, but here she trains her eye on the question of power and who wields it—and through what means. In exploring these questions, Sainz Borgo raises the stakes unbearably high. In my translation, I have tried to reflect those raised stakes in rhythmically impactful, often short sentences, while also creating breathing room for the vivid images of Sainz Borgo's metaphors.

Perhaps the most notable difference in this second novel is the introduction of a speculative element, that of the amnesia epidemic that sets into motion the migration and the events of the book. As I worked on this translation, I found myself listening for echoes of reality, and paying attention to the ways in which this reality is both reflected and refracted in the novel. The challenge was to ensure these echoes were present for readers of the translation, while only ever remaining just that—echoes. It was a fine line to walk, ensuring the translation had the truth effect of a particular time and place without making it of that time and place.

Most of all, I have tried to convey Angustias's voice, resilient even in her grief; Visitación's joie de vivre, defiance, and irreverence; and Consuelo's vulnerability.

—Elizabeth Bryer

Here ends Karina Sainz Borgo's
No Place to Bury the Dead.

The first edition of this book was printed
and bound at Lakeside Book Company
in Harrisonburg, Virginia, in November 2024.

A NOTE ON THE TYPE

The text of this novel was set in Perpetua, a serif typeface designed by Eric Gill for Monotype in 1925. Commissioned by Stanley Morrison, an influential printing historian and advisor for Monotype, Gill mined his experience as a sculptor and stonemason to create a crisp, clean, and contemporary font. Named for the Christian martyr Vibia Perpetua, the typeface enjoys high popularity in book printing and is commonly used for covers and page headings.

HarperVia

An imprint dedicated to publishing international voices, offering readers a chance to encounter other lives and other points of view via the language of the imagination.